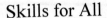

The great horse-racing season in Canada is about to begin. Owners from all over the world will travel across the country, from Toronto to Vancouver, on a special train – and Filmer will be on it. Filmer, and friends.

There is only one way to stop him. Someone else must join the train and watch – and be ready to act . . .

Dick Francis is one of the most successful thriller writers in the world. He did not begin to write until after a career in horse-racing, as one of the top riders in Britain.

He was born in Wales in 1920, into a farming and horse-loving family, and learned to ride as soon as he could walk. His only ambition was to race horses but his plans were interrupted by World War II. He joined the Royal Air Force and flew both fighters and bombers, and only seriously began his racing career in 1946.

Later, when his injuries forced him to retire, he began working as a racing journalist but soon discovered he could raise his income through writing novels. His first novel, *Dead Cert* (1962), sold well and his second, *Nerve* (1964), did even better. Francis used his knowledge of the racing world to create strong, believable stories. Since the sixties, he has written about one book a year, all of them praised by critics.

The following titles are available at Levels 4, 5 and 6:

For a complete list of the titles available in the Penguin Readers series please write to the following address for a catalogue: Penguin ELT Marketing Department, Penguin Books Ltd, 27 Wrights Lane, London w8 5tz.

The Edge

DICK FRANCIS

Level 6

Retold by Robin Waterfield
Series Editor: Derek Strange

PENGUIN BOOKS

PENGUIN BOOKS

Published by the Penguin Group
Penguin Books Ltd, 27 Wrights Lane, London W8 5TZ, England
Penguin Books USA Inc., 375 Hudson Street, New York, New York 10014, USA
Penguin Books Australia Ltd, Ringwood, Victoria, Australia
Penguin Books Canada Ltd, 10 Alcorn Avenue, Toronto, Ontario, Canada M4V 3B2
Penguin Books (NZ) Ltd, 182–190 Wairau Road, Auckland 10, New Zealand

Penguin Books Ltd, Registered Offices: Harmondsworth, Middlesex, England

The Edge by Dick Francis
Copyright © Dick Francis 1988
This adaptation published by Penguin Books in 1992
3 5 7 9 10 8 6 4 2

Text copyright © Robin Waterfield 1992
Illustrations copyright © Piers Sandford 1992
All rights reserved

The moral right of the adapter and of the illustrator has been asserted

Illustrations by Piers Sandford

Printed in England by Clays Ltd, St Ives plc
Set in 11/13½ pt Lasercomp Bembo

To the teacher:

In addition to all the language forms of Levels One to Five, which are used again at this level of the series, the main verb forms and tenses used at Level Six are:

- future perfect verbs, passives with continuous or perfect aspects of the 'third' conditional with continuous forms
- modal verbs: *needn't* and *needn't have* (to express absence of necessity), *would* (to describe habitual past actions), *should* and *should have* (to express probability or failed expectation), *may have* and *might have* (to express possibility), *could have* and *would have* (to express past, unfulfilled possibility or likelihood).

Also used are:

- non–defining relative clauses.

Specific attention is paid to vocabulary development in the Vocabulary Work exercises at the end of the book. These exercises are aimed at training students to enlarge their vocabulary systematically through intelligent reading and effective use of a dictionary.

To the student:

Dictionary Words:

- As you read this book, you will find that some words are in darker black ink than the others on the page. Look them up in your dictionary, if you do not already know them, or try to guess the meaning of the words first, and then look them up later, to check.

CHAPTER ONE

I was following Derry Welfram at a race meeting when he dropped to the ground and lay face down in the mud in the light rain. Several people walked straight past him, thinking that he was drunk. I knew that he wasn't drunk, because I'd been following him all afternoon – and, in fact, for some days. However, I didn't go up to see what was wrong or to try to help him: I didn't want anyone to see me with Welfram.

It was soon clear that this was not just an unconscious drunk. A doctor came out of the race track building, turned Welfram over, did some tests and started to hit him hard on the chest. He carried on at this for a while, but eventually gave up. An ambulance arrived and took Welfram's body away.

I headed for the bar: that was where the gossip would be. I moved around the room, listening, and it wasn't long before I overheard a woman ask her husband whether he'd heard about that man who died of a heart attack earlier.

It was a pity, I thought, that Welfram had died – not because anyone would miss him, but because it put me and my boss, Brigadier Valentine Catto, back to where we started. The investigation had got nowhere so far.

My name is Tor Kelsey. I work for the Jockey Club★ as a kind of policeman – or some would say as a spy. The horse-racing world is attractive to criminals, and our job is to catch

★ A jockey rides horses in races. The Jockey Club looks after the interests of horse-racing.

them and warn them off, if possible, or get them banned from any further involvement in horse-racing. On extreme occasions, we bring in the official police force.

One of the worst criminals to inhabit the horse-racing world was Julius Apollo Filmer. Tall and elegant, he mixed with the highest levels of society, because they were the ones with the money and the horses. Nobody knew exactly how he did it, but he managed to persuade people to sell him their best horses cheaply. You have to understand that a prizewinning horse is worth millions. So why would people sell? The paperwork was all nice and legal, but something rotten was in the air. We were certain that Filmer used **blackmail** and threats, but we needed hard evidence.

A few months ago, we almost had the evidence. A young **groom** foolishly boasted in a pub that what he knew could spell big trouble for Mr Julius Filmer. Two days later, the groom turned up dead in a ditch. The police found four witnesses to pin the planning of the crime on Filmer, but on the day of the trial they either left the country or changed their stories, with the result that Filmer got off. Once again, Filmer's threats and blackmail had proved successful, and justice had failed to be done.

However, one of the frightened witnesses hinted to Catto (who could be rather persuasive himself) that it was Welfram who had threatened him, until he changed his story. So Catto gave me the job of finding out all I could about Welfram, with a view to proving that he was Filmer's man. But now Welfram was dead.

A few days later, Catto asked to see me and we met at his club. We discussed Welfram's death for a while, but he soon came to the point.

'Have you ever heard of the **Transcontinental** Race Train?' he asked.

'Yes,' I said. I'd spent some months in Canada. 'Owners from all over the world take their horses to Canada and travel right across the country, in considerable luxury, stopping here and there to enter their horses in races. It's a famous event in Canada. But why do you ask?'

'Filmer's going on it this year,' Catto replied. 'In fact, it looks as though he's made special arrangements in order to go on it: he recently bought a half share in a horse that was already entered for the train. It seems that he is up to something. He's still angry about the trial: he has threatened to hit back at the world's racing authorities – for **persecuting** him, he says.'

'If anyone ever deserved persecution, he does,' I said. 'But what on earth could he do on the train?'

'That's for you to discover,' Catto said. 'I've contacted the head of the Canadian Jockey Club – an old friend of mine called Bill Baudelaire – and he's arranged for a place for you on the train.'

'I hope you remembered to buy me a horse as well,' I joked, 'otherwise they'll soon find out that I'm not an owner and get suspicious.'

Catto laughed. 'Don't worry,' he said. 'In fact, other people go on the train as well, not just owners. People go just to attend the races and have a good holiday. Of course, these racegoers don't travel as luxuriously as the owners . . .'

'Oh, great!' I said sarcastically. 'Thanks for a ten-day, uncomfortable journey!'

'No, no!' exclaimed Catto. 'You're not going as a racegoer. They travel in a different part of the train from the owners, so you wouldn't be able to keep an eye on Filmer.'

'Well, what *am* I going as, then?' I asked.

'As a waiter,' Catto said. He smiled at my surprise, and added, 'These rich people hardly notice waiters: you'll be well placed to listen and spy.' Then he brought the conversation to an end. 'You're due to meet Baudelaire in Ottawa – he'll tell you more. Oh, and Tor – take care: Filmer's a murderer.'

CHAPTER TWO

I started on this line of work a few years ago. I had been travelling the world for several years, working anywhere I could and at any job, although the jobs were often connected with horses. I had been brought up by a horse-mad aunt after my parents had died when I was still a child.

I came back to England when I was twenty-five and had a meeting with Clement Cornborough, a lawyer who was an old friend of the family. He took me to lunch and we just made small talk, as far as I could tell.

Two days later, however, he rang me up and invited me to dinner, this time at his club. It turned out that a third person had also been invited to dinner – his old friend and fellow club-member, Brigadier Valentine Catto. Catto was very much the soldier, but by no means given to hasty action: that evening, for the first time (but by no means the last), I heard Catto's famous and typical saying, 'Thought before action'.

Catto wasn't obvious, but he was definitely asking me questions about my life. By the time dinner was half over, it was clear to me that I was being interviewed for something, though I didn't know what. I only learned much later that Catto had once happened to mention to Cornborough that what the Jockey Club really needed was an invisible man – someone who knew the horse-racing world well, but who wasn't known in return, an eyes and ears man, a fly on the wall of horse-racing who no one would notice. A person like this, they thought, was unlikely to be found.

And then two weeks later, I flew in from Mexico and met Cornborough. During lunch, the idea came to him that perhaps I was the man Catto was looking for.

By the end of that evening at the club, I had a job.

◆

I flew to Ottawa the day after my meeting with Catto and went straight from the airport to Baudelaire's office, which overlooked the city and was full of antique wooden furniture. He was about forty years old, with red hair and blue eyes. We took to each other straight away. After chatting for a while, to get to know each other, I asked him what he could tell me about the owner of the horse which Filmer now partly owned.

'It's a woman,' he replied, 'with the extraordinary name of Daffodil Quentin. Her husband was a respected member of the Canadian racing world, and when he died a year ago, he left her all his horses – and everything else as well. Since then, no fewer than three of the horses have suddenly died, and Mrs Quentin has been paid all the insurance.'

'You mean . . . ?' I said.

'We're not certain of anything,' Baudelaire replied to my unspoken question. 'But it does rather look like insurance fraud. We've no proof, however. And now she and Filmer are partners!'

'An unholy pair,' I remarked.

'Exactly.'

'What's the name of the horse?'

'Laurentide Ice,' Baudelaire said. 'It's named after a famous Canadian **glacier**. God, I wish I knew what those two were planning!'

'Leave it to me,' I said, but I didn't feel as confident as I tried to sound.

Baudelaire and I arranged to meet the next day, after I'd had time to digest what he'd told me, and to read the **brochure** he'd given me, all about the Transcontinental Race Train. I went through the brochure during breakfast in my hotel.

The train, I learned, was basically divided into three parts. The front four carriages would hold the luggage, the horses and the grooms; the next five provided accommodation for the racegoers. It was the final five carriages which concerned me most.

First, there were the sleeping **compartments** for the staff – waiters (including me), cooks, travel agent and other officials of the railway. Then, the next two carriages consisted of the extremely luxurious sleeping compartments for the owners. Lastly, there was the first-class dining-car and a carriage with a bar for the owners to sit in when they were not eating meals. The overall impression was one of great style and luxury: no expense had been spared. And one would undoubtedly have to be very wealthy to buy a ticket for the Transcontinental Race Train.

The train would travel west, from Toronto to Vancouver. Apart from short stops for the engine to take on fuel, and for more food and water to be taken on board, there was to be an overnight stop in Winnipeg, in a top-class hotel, with a special horse-race laid on, and generous prize money for the winner. Another special attraction would be staying in a hotel in the mountains: the hotel brochure promised amazing views of natural beauty, including a glacier. Then the train would descend to Vancouver, on the west coast, where the trip would end with another horse-race. It sounded like one long party – and it sounded as though being a waiter was going to be hard work.

The Transcontinental Race Train had been running once a

year for several years by now, and the races attracted huge crowds. People flooded into Winnipeg and Vancouver from all over Canada – not to say from all over the world – and the regular transcontinental train, called the Canadian, followed the Race Train all the way across Canada, bringing extra racegoers who couldn't afford the cost of a place on the Race Train itself.

CHAPTER THREE

Bill Baudelaire came to my hotel room in the middle of the morning. I ordered coffee, and he filled me in on some further details.

I asked him why he hadn't simply blocked Filmer's place on the Race Train.

'Believe me,' he said, 'if I could have, I would have. I rang Catto to ask what I could do. Were there any grounds for banning Filmer, I asked? He said that there was no firm evidence. If he'd ever been found guilty of anything, even a parking ticket ... But he hadn't, so anything I could have done to keep Filmer off the train would have been illegal; Filmer could have protested that he was being persecuted, and more people would have believed him. So I asked Catto whether, since we couldn't get Filmer *off* the train, we could get one of our men *on* the train. Here in Canada we don't have anyone quite like you in our Jockey Club. So here you are. I hope you're as good as Catto says you are.'

I murmured something modest.

'One thing our brochure doesn't mention, Tor,' Baudelaire went on, 'is that we allow anyone who owns his own private rail car to apply for it to be joined on to the train. This year, unusually, we had an applicant: Mercer Lorrimore.'

He sat back in his chair, looking satisfied with himself. He had spoken the name as if I should recognize it, but I must have looked blank. He raised an eyebrow. 'Don't tell me I have to explain who Mercer Lorrimore is,' he said.

'I'm afraid so,' I answered.

'He's only about the richest man in Canada,' said Baudelaire. 'Most of his money comes from banking. He and his family are known all over Canada; the society and gossip columns of the magazines and newspapers would be lost without them. Whatever else anyone can say about him, though, no one can deny that Mercer loves horses and horse-racing. He has some wonderful horses.'

'And he's coming on your train,' I said.

'Yes,' said Baudelaire, 'and so is the rest of his family too – his wife Bambi, their son Sheridan, who's about twenty, and their teenage daughter Xanthe.'

'And you say they'll have a separate car,' I said.

'Yes, it'll be added on to the rear of the train.'

'One other thing,' I said, 'before I forget. How will I get in touch with you, if I need to? I don't want to ring your office at the Jockey Club, because the fewer Club members who know that I'm on the train, the better. Can I ring you at home?'

'I wouldn't advise that,' he said. 'My three daughters are never off the phone. Why don't you ring my mother? She'll pass messages on to me; I'll be sure to tell her where I'll be. She's always at home, because she's **bedridden**.'

'All right,' I said, 'if you say so.' He wrote the number down on a piece of paper and gave it to me. But I wasn't particularly happy, since I imagined that a bedridden old woman would have a leaky memory, and be slightly deaf, and so on.

♦

My last visit in Ottawa, before leaving for Toronto, was to the office of the travel company who were arranging the whole trip. Since I was to be disguised as a waiter on the train, it had been necessary to let someone in their office in on the secret – without letting them know exactly what my job was. It was the travel agent who would accompany the passengers throughout the trip who had been told. Her name was Nell Richmond. I soon found her desk in the office and introduced myself. She had fair hair and grey eyes and was about my age – between twenty-five and thirty. I was immediately glad she was going to be on the train.

Our conversation was constantly interrupted by the telephone on her desk ringing. She coped with all the calls in a calm, efficient manner, her eyes occasionally meeting mine with a kind of humorous or curious look, as if to learn about me. But between phone calls I managed to find out where in Toronto I should report to pick up my waiter's uniform, and she gave me a pass to get on the train.

'I don't really know what you're doing,' she said, 'and I'm not sure I want to know. But Mr Baudelaire was most insistent that I should give you any information you want. What can I tell you?'

All about yourself, I thought, but said out loud: 'Do you have a plan of who sleeps where?'

'Certainly,' she said. She pulled it out of her file and gave it to me. 'Anything else?'

'No, I don't think so,' I said. 'Oh, you could tell me if this is complete.'

I showed her a list I'd drawn up of all the staff and owners who would be in the end carriages of the train. She checked it carefully, occasionally brushing her hair out of her eyes.

'I've nothing to add to that,' she said. 'But there is one new

15

arrival, further up the train. Baudelaire rang a short while ago to say that he had arranged for a woman called Leslie Brown to check who comes and goes in the horse-car. Only owners and grooms are allowed in. The horses aren't in any danger, are they?'

'I wish I knew,' I said.

CHAPTER FOUR

Early the next morning, Nell and I caught a train together to Toronto, since the Race Train was due to leave in the evening. During the journey, we chatted about this and that – her job, my job, her ambition to become a writer, and so on. Of course, each of us made sure that the other was not married! I also made sure that she would not tell anyone else on the Race Train what my job was – as much as she knew about it.

'Nell,' I had asked, 'are you good at keeping secrets?'

'I keep half a dozen every day before breakfast,' she replied. 'Why? What secret do you want me to keep?'

'It's very important that no one on the train knows that I am not what I seem to be – a waiter,' I said. 'I mean, there may be one or two other people who have to know, but I must be the one to tell them. And that means not only that you mustn't say anything, but also that you'll have to be careful not to give me away by anything you do – any look on your face, or something like that. OK?'

'OK,' she agreed. 'You're a real mystery man.'

We parted at the station not just as good friends, but something more: there was a strong attraction between us, which we had both been deliberately feeding with the occasional approving glance and with the light and easy mood of our conversation. I kissed her goodbye on the cheek, and she left to go about her travel agent's business.

I made my way to the uniform centre and was measured up for a waiter's uniform. I was given a grey jacket, two pairs of grey trousers, five white shirts, two gold **waistcoats**, and two striped ties in the railway company's colours. I particularly admired myself in a waistcoat.

The Race Train was already standing at the platform, so I went there, boarded and introduced myself to the rest of the crew. The head waiter was a small Frenchman called Emil.

'Have you ever worked in a restaurant?' he asked.

'No, I haven't.'

'Never mind,' he said. 'I'll show you how to set places, and give you only easy jobs to do. Even so, we'll appreciate the extra help.'

He gave me a copy of the train's timetable, explaining that I should learn it by heart, since the most common question passengers ask is where and when the next stop is. Passengers expect anyone in a uniform to know absolutely everything about the train, he said. Then he introduced me to the rest of the dining-car staff – Cathy and Oliver, my fellow waiters; Angus, the Scottish cook; and Simone, Angus's assistant.

'The first job,' Emil announced, 'is to prepare for a drinks party when the passengers board. We have half an hour, so come on.'

I asked Emil to show me first where my sleeping compartment was, so that I could change into my uniform. Then I returned to the dining-car and helped the others.

The Race Train was so famous that a large crowd of people came just to watch the fortunate few board.

Julius Filmer was among the first to arrive, looking as elegant as usual in a long grey coat and a patterned silk scarf.

He came with a woman who could only be Daffodil Quentin: when you are no longer young and you have a name like that, I thought, you are bound to colour your hair blonde. You are bound to wear too much make-up and show off your expensive fur coat even when it's a warm evening.

Most of the passengers went to their bedrooms first, before coming to the dining-car for the drinks party. The dining-car was rapidly filling up and I was busy serving **champagne** when the Lorrimores made their entrance. Mercer Lorrimore and his wife Bambi looked quite ordinary: only their clothes and perfect haircuts announced their wealth. Behind them were a young man and a **sulky** teenage girl – Sheridan and Xanthe, their children.

'Where do we sit?' Mercer asked me.

'Anywhere you like, sir,' I said.

They saw an unoccupied table and made their way towards it. Sheridan pushed past an elderly couple, nearly spilling their champagne, and sat down, saying in a loud voice, 'I don't see why we have to sit in here when we have our own private car.' Mercer told him to be quiet and to behave; Bambi and Xanthe stared out of the window – whether in boredom or embarrassment, it was hard to tell.

Soon the car was full. Julius and Daffodil shared a table with the elderly couple, Mr and Mrs Young. I listened to their conversation as much as I could, but it was all perfectly innocent.

Nell was acting the efficient hostess, making sure that everyone was happy and calling them all by name. Only the Lorrimores were sitting in silence, while everyone else was chatting and getting to know one another. At one point, Nell passed me as I was coming out of the kitchen with more drinks.

I looked at her with admiration. 'You're wonderful,' I said.
'Yes, aren't I?' she replied with a smile.

CHAPTER FIVE

After the party, the train set off and I had no more time for
spying. There was washing up to do, then laying the tables
and serving a meal – then more washing up! It seemed that a
waiter's job was never over. I felt that I had to tell Emil that I
was not a regular waiter, and that there may be times when I
would neglect my job as a waiter. He gave me a strange look,
but admitted that he had had his suspicions, ever since the rail
company had insisted on him taking an inexperienced person
on as a waiter.

As soon as my work was finished, I decided I should check
up on the horses. I walked unsteadily up the train, past all the
racegoers in their carriages, and was stopped by the locked
door of the horse-car.

I knocked on the door. A slight woman, aged about forty
and dressed for business in jeans, boots and a white short-
sleeved shirt, put her head around the door, took one look at
my waiter's uniform, and told me that I was not allowed in
the horse-car. Before I could protest or say anything else, she
had shut the door and locked it again.

I realized I needed some higher authority. Of course, the
conductor* – I should introduce myself to him anyway. I
made my way back down the train as far as his office and
found him in. I told him a little about myself, and showed
him a letter from Bill Baudelaire which said that I was
working for him.

* A conductor is an officer of the railway who is in charge of the train
during its journey.

19

'All right,' said the conductor, whose name was George Burley. 'What can I do for you?'

'Several things,' I said. 'But first I want to inspect the horse-car.'

George understood at once, and laughed. 'So you've met the fierce Ms Leslie Brown,' he said. 'She would like to rule the whole train, I think. OK, I'll see what I can do. Let's go.'

I liked his dry sense of humour. Back at the horse-car, George told Ms Brown firmly that I could go wherever I wanted on the train, and that he would be responsible for my actions. She looked at me disapprovingly, but let me in with George. It was only when I stroked the horses' noses and gave them some sugar lumps from my pocket that she began to warm to me at all.

There was nothing out of the ordinary in the horse-car. The space was nearly all filled by the horses' boxes, and the food containers and huge water tank, which supplied all the horses. Laurentide Ice was the only grey, I noticed. I looked around until I was satisfied that I knew the arrangements; then George and I returned to his office, which also doubled as his bedroom and the train's radio room.

'Now what?' he asked.

'There's only one thing I need to know at the moment,' I said. 'Does the train have a telephone?'

'Sure,' he said. 'It's right here.' He opened a drawer and produced the phone. 'But, as you can see,' he went on, 'it's a radio phone.'

'So . . . ?' I asked.

'So it only works near cities, where they have the equipment for receiving and sending signals. Moreover, it's very expensive to make a call on it, so the passengers generally prefer to wait until we stop at a station, and then use the pay phones there.'

'But it would be more private for me to use your phone here in your office,' I pointed out. 'Would that be OK with you?'

'Sure,' he said. 'Anything for a bit of excitement.'

By the time I got back to the bar, it was quite late. All the passengers had gone to bed, except for Xanthe Lorrimore and Mrs Young. Xanthe was sitting at one table, staring sulkily at nothing – unless it was her own reflection in the window. Mrs Young was reading a book at another table.

'Bring me a Coke*,' Xanthe ordered, as soon as she saw me.

'Certainly, miss.'

When I brought it, I explained that she would have to pay cash for it, since drinks from the bar were not included in the price of the train fare.

'But that's silly,' she said, annoyed. 'Anyway, I haven't got any money on me.'

'Oh, do let me pay, dear,' said Mrs Young, who had overheard our conversation. 'And why don't you come and sit with me?' she asked Xanthe.

Xanthe may have been sulking, but she was also clearly lonely. She moved to Mrs Young's table; I stood near by while Mrs Young looked for her purse in her handbag.

'You've been deep in thought, dear,' said Mrs Young kindly to Xanthe. 'Can I help?'

It was as if her question unlocked something. 'I doubt you can help,' Xanthe said. 'It's just that I don't want to be on this train really – I've got better things to do. Nor does Sheridan, for that matter. But Daddy insisted on both of us coming, so that he can keep an eye on us, he says, and be sure what we're doing at any moment of the day. And it's all Sheridan's fault – if he were anyone else's child, he'd be in prison.'

* Coca-Cola.

The words had spilled out as if by themselves, and even Xanthe looked surprised. 'I . . . I don't mean exactly that,' she stammered.

But that was exactly what she had meant.

CHAPTER SIX

Mrs Young paid me and said I needn't stay up. I left, thinking about how unhappy Xanthe was. She looked like a confused, miserable teenager.

Next afternoon, when the train stopped at Sudbury, I seized the opportunity to use George's radio phone. I rang the number Bill Baudelaire had given me. The woman's voice at the other end sounded very light and young.

'Could I speak to Mrs Baudelaire, please?' I said.

'Speaking.'

'I mean . . . the older Mrs Baudelaire.'

'Any Mrs Baudelaire who is older than me is in her grave,' she said. 'Who are you?'

'Tor Kelsey.'

'Oh yes,' she replied instantly. 'The invisible man. Do you have any messages for Bill? I'll write them down.'

'Yes,' I said. 'Thank you. Could you ask him for any information about a Mr and Mrs Young, who own a horse called Sparrowgrass? And ask him if Sheridan Lorrimore has ever been in the kind of trouble that could have landed him in prison.'

'My dear,' she said drily, 'the Lorrimores don't go to prison.'

'So I understand,' I said. 'Oh, and one more thing. Ask Bill which of the horses on the train are running at Winnipeg and Vancouver, and which ones have the best chance of winning either race.'

'I don't need to ask Bill that,' said Mrs Baudelaire confidently. 'All the horses are running at Vancouver, which is the main event; Sparrowgrass or the Lorrimores' Voting Right will win. Laurentide Ice will start strongly, but slow down later in the race. As for the Winnipeg race, no one else stands much of a chance, because Mercer Lorrimore is transporting his great horse Premiere in by road.'

I was impressed. She explained that she and her husband – who was now dead – had owned Canada's top racing newspaper for years, so she knew what she was talking about.

'Mrs Baudelaire,' I said, 'you are priceless.'

'I agree,' she said with a laugh. 'Anything else?'

'No. I'll ring you again from Winnipeg tomorrow evening. And . . . er . . . I hope you're well.'

'No, I'm not,' she said, 'but thank you for asking. Goodbye, young man. I'm always here.'

She put down the phone quickly as if to stop me from asking further questions about her illness. And I had completely changed my mind about bedridden old women.

About an hour after we'd left Sudbury, we stopped for about five minutes at a place called Cartier and then went on again. The passengers had eaten dinner and were drinking coffee or drifting away to the bar. Xanthe Lorrimore got up from her table after a while and left – only to come back screaming and obviously badly scared.

'What is it?' asked her parents in alarm. Even Sheridan looked interested.

'I was nearly killed,' she cried.

'What do you mean?'

'Our private car,' she said. 'It's gone! I opened the connecting door and nearly stepped off into space! And that other train, the Canadian, is right behind us, isn't it? It'll crash into our car . . . and . . . and we could have been in it! Don't you see?'

23

'Our private car,' she said. 'It's gone! I opened the connecting door and nearly stepped off into space!'

The Lorrimores and nearly everyone else ran off to look; Mrs Young stayed with Xanthe. Once I had checked on the truth of what Xanthe had said, I went to find George.

'Quick!' I said. 'Your radio. The Lorrimores' car has been **unhitched** and the Canadian is coming!'

He left me on the radio, while he ran up the train to tell the driver to stop. Soon, I felt the train slowing down and stopping. In the meantime, I had contacted a town up ahead called Schreiber, and the radioman there had signalled the Canadian to stop; he had got through to the train before it passed through Cartier. We began to reverse slowly back down the track.

The Lorrimores' car was found not far outside Cartier. George went to make his inspection and to attend to the rejoining of the carriage. He returned an hour later with anger on his face.

'What's the matter?' I asked.

'Nothing,' he said violently. 'That's what the matter is. There was nothing wrong with the Lorrimores' car at all.'

'What do you mean?'

'That was no accident,' he said. 'The car was unhitched on purpose. The steam heat pipe wasn't broken: it had been unlocked. Now, it is not easy to unhitch a carriage: it takes a few minutes, even for someone who knows what to do. So it must have been done at Cartier, when we were stopped. And then whoever did it must have found a way to disguise the fact that the carriage was actually unhitched: he must have joined it to the rest of the train with a piece of rope or something. He knew that the rope would break after a while and then the Lorrimores' car would have been left standing on the track. He knew that the Canadian was coming up behind us. Canada is so large that the only economical thing to do is have a single railway track across most of it, except at stations; there would have been no chance of the Canadian changing to another track.'

'What would have happened?' I asked.

'It's difficult to say exactly,' George replied. 'The Canadian would certainly have destroyed the Lorrimores' car. If anyone had been in it, they would have been killed. The Canadian itself might have been knocked off the rails, which would have caused a great deal of expensive damage, certainly some injuries to the passengers, and possibly some deaths. But do you know what the worst thing about all this is?'

'What?'

'Well, I'll put it this way. Would you know how to unhitch a railway carriage?'

'No, of course not.'

'Exactly,' said George. 'It was an expert job. It was **sabotage** – and it could only have been done by a railwayman. That makes me feel . . . I don't know . . . betrayed. I love the railway: I can't understand any railwayman wanting to damage any part of it.'

CHAPTER SEVEN

I left him to write his report on the act of sabotage. Back in the dining-car, Xanthe was feeling better, as a result of being the centre of sympathetic attention, and people were recovering their party mood. They didn't appreciate the seriousness of the situation. As far as they were concerned, no one was hurt, and it must have been an accident.

Filmer was sitting with Mercer Lorrimore, telling him to take the railway company to court for their neglect. Bambi was at the same table, pretending to be interested in the men's conversation.

Xanthe was being comforted mainly by Mrs Young, but

every time anyone passed her table, they asked how she was feeling.

Nell was sitting with a middle-aged couple who owned a horse called Redi-Hot. As I bent across the table to wipe it, she whispered jokingly, 'If you're a good little waiter, I'll give you a tip,' and then ordered her drink in a louder voice which the others could hear.

After I'd delivered her drink, Sheridan Lorrimore loudly demanded that I bring him a glass of wine.

'You know you're not supposed to have alcohol,' his sister protested.

'Mind your own business,' he said, and then to me, 'Get it!'

'Don't get it,' said Xanthe.

Uncertain whom to obey, I stayed where I was. Sheridan stood up in a temper and pushed me roughly towards the bar. 'Do as I say,' he said. 'Go on!'

As I left, I heard him laugh and say, 'You have to kick them about, you know.'

His father followed me into the bar. 'I apologize for my son's behaviour,' he said tiredly, as if he'd done so hundreds of times before. 'I hope this will help.' He took twenty dollars out of his wallet and offered it to me.

'Please don't,' I said. 'There's no need.'

'Yes, yes. Take it,' he insisted.

I saw that he would feel better if I took it, as if paying money would help to excuse the act. I thought that he should stop trying to buy pardons for his son, and pay for medical treatment instead. But then, perhaps he already had. There was more wrong with Sheridan than a bad temper, and it must have been obvious to his father for a long time.

I didn't want to accept the money, but this matter had already made me more visible than I wanted to be, so it was best to take the money and get it all over with.

When I returned to the dining-car, Mercer had sat down next to Filmer again and their heads were close. I wondered whether this had been one of Filmer's aims – to get close to Lorrimore. If it was, what was the point of it? What *was* the man up to? And had he arranged the accident with the Lorrimores' car especially so that he could get close to Mercer Lorrimore?

It was by now nearly midnight. The Youngs were standing up in the dining-room, ready to go to bed. But Xanthe was alarmed at the departure of her new friend and was begging to be moved from the private car. Nell said that there was a spare bed and Xanthe could hardly wait to move her things in there. I doubted she would set foot in the private car again for the whole journey: she had been thoroughly frightened.

The Lorrimores left without even saying goodnight to their daughter. Sheridan gave his mother a look of hatred when she ordered him to bed.

'There's no love lost in that family,' Nell said to me when we were alone in the dining-car. 'Mercer's nice but has something weighing heavily on his mind; Bambi is bitter; Xanthe's all mixed up; and I don't know what to make of Sheridan. Did you know that both he and Xanthe were given millions of dollars by their grandmother?'

'I didn't know that,' I said. 'He's either just a spoiled young man with a quick temper, or . . .'

'Or what?' Nell asked. 'I never quite know what you're thinking.'

'I was thinking how you hold your file in front of your chest,' I said, 'as if to defend yourself?'

'Defend myself?' she said. 'Against you?' But all the same, she put the file down.

'And I was thinking,' I continued, 'that it's a pity I'm a waiter.'

'Why?'

'Because a waiter can't kiss you,' I said.

'I'll consider myself kissed,' she said. 'And now goodnight. Aren't you going to bed?'

'Soon.'

'You mean, when everything's . . . safe?'

'You might say so.'

'What exactly does the Jockey Club expect you to do?'

'See trouble before it comes.'

'But that's almost impossible.'

'True,' I said, thinking about the Lorrimores' carriage. 'But weren't you on your way to bed?'

She smiled.

'So goodnight,' I said gently, and off she went with a glance over her shoulder at me.

I went into the bar just as Filmer and Daffodil were leaving, and just in time to hear the end of one of Filmer's sentences: '. . . when we get to Winnipeg.'

'You mean Vancouver,' Daffodil said. 'You're always confusing Winnipeg and Vancouver.'

CHAPTER EIGHT

The next day, I overheard a curious echo of this conversation between Filmer and Daffodil. We were stopped at midday in a town called Thunder Bay, and as usual all the passengers were getting some fresh air out on the platform.

I saw Julius Filmer walking determinedly up the platform, towards the front of the train. I decided to keep up with him, but from the inside of the train: apart from anything else, it was warmer inside! I thought at first that he was just taking an open-air route to his own bedroom, but he carried on past that carriage. He was going to see his horse, no doubt.

About half-way up the train, however, he was stopped by a thin-faced man. They started to talk to each other, but to my annoyance I couldn't hear what they were saying, and I couldn't understand their hand signals on their own. But then their discussion became more heated and they began to raise their voices.

'I said before Vancouver,' Filmer shouted at Thin-face.

'You said before Winnipeg,' Thin-face shouted back, 'and I've done it, and I want my money.'

Just then they were interrupted by the awful Daffodil, who wanted Filmer to accompany her to see Laurentide Ice. I silently cursed her: it had been getting interesting. What else could they have been talking about other than the sabotage on the Lorrimores' car? Filmer and Daffodil walked away up towards the horse-car. Thin-face crossed the tracks by the foot-bridge and went over to the main station.

I badly wanted a photograph of Thin-face to show to Baudelaire. I ran back to my room and fetched my camera. But just as I was getting into position to take a picture, the Canadian pulled into the station. It stopped on the track between me and the station, and perfectly blocked my view of Thin-face.

I cursed my bad luck and again cursed Daffodil for interrupting the conversation. But perhaps I shouldn't curse Daffodil. The thought entered my mind that she and Filmer would be at least fifteen minutes walking to the horse-car, inspecting their pride and joy, and then walking back again. This could be the opportunity I'd been waiting for: Filmer was away, and the train was fairly empty.

I returned my camera to my room and then carried on down the train until I reached Filmer's room. I looked both ways up and down the corridor to make sure no one was watching me, took a deep breath and opened the door. If I'd paused for more thought, I perhaps wouldn't have had the nerve, but I was inside! A quick search of his drawers and cupboard showed nothing interesting or important. I dropped to my knees and looked under his bed. There was a shiny, black, leather **briefcase** there. I pulled it out and placed it on the bed. It was locked, of course, with the type of lock which relied on a series of numbers; the left-hand lock used three numbers, and the right-hand one another three.

How long did I have before Filmer came back? Might he not even now be outside in the corridor? What if someone else came in – a member of staff, for instance? What possible excuse would I have? None at all. The very thought made me begin to sweat. I wiped my hands on my trousers and turned to the right-hand wheels.

The right-hand wheels were set at 137. I set to work, going upward through the numbers: 138, 139, 140 . . . I was listening for the tiny difference in noise that might indicate when the numbers were correct; but I was also testing the lock by hand, to make sure. My fingers shook: 147, 148, 149 . . . My face was sweating . . . 150, 151 . . .

The lock flew open at 151. I could hardly believe my luck. But how long had it taken me? I had lost track of time. The danger was great, but I had to see if the left-hand lock was set to the same number. No, it wasn't; I decided not to try the left-hand wheels any more. I rolled all six wheels back to their original numbers and silently left the room.

◆

Later I described Thin-face to George, but he didn't recognize him and couldn't say whether he was on the train.

'We did have a bad man on board once,' he said. 'A couple of years ago, it must have been. As a matter of fact, he was a waiter, like you.'

'What did he do?' I asked.

'He tried to put drugs in everyone's food,' said George.

I had an idea. 'George,' I said, 'do all the horses share the food I saw in the horse-car, or do any of them have their own special food?'

'Yes,' he replied, 'one of them does. The groom gives his horse special food from bags labelled "Sunday evening", "Monday morning", and so on. He was showing them to me.'

'Which horse?' I asked.

'The one belonging to Mrs Quentin,' said George. 'The groom said one of her horses died recently from the wrong food, so she was being extra cautious.'

CHAPTER NINE

In Winnipeg, the horses were taken off the train and to the racetrack for the next day's race. Buses were waiting to take the passengers to their hotels. Staff like myself had to make their own way to their cheaper hotels.

As soon as I had checked into my room, I rang Mrs Baudelaire.

'I've got answers to your questions,' she said. 'Ready?'

'Yes.'

'There's nothing at all suspicious about the Youngs: they're just a nice Canadian couple, popular with everyone and welcome at every race meeting.'

'Thanks,' I said, 'that's what I thought, and certainly what I hoped, but I had to check. What about Sheridan Lorrimore?'

'Well, this is a bit shocking,' she said. 'Such a fine old Canadian family! But Sheridan seems to have been **expelled** from Cambridge University last May. It's all very mysterious: no one quite knows why he was expelled. Bill says to tell you that Brigadier Catto is trying to find out. Does that make sense to you?'

'Yes, thank you,' I said. 'Are you going to speak to Bill before he flies to Winnipeg for the race?'

'I wasn't planning to, but I can.'

'Could you tell him to expect delivery at the racetrack of a small packet from me? It will contain some of the horses' food which I want analysed.'

'That sounds alarming,' she said. 'Don't worry, I'll let him know.'

'And last, but not least,' I said, 'can you ask him to ask Catto if the numbers 151 mean anything to Filmer. For example, they might form part of his phone number or his car number-plate or something. They should be the last three numbers in a series of six numbers. Have you got all that?'

'Yes,' said Mrs Baudelaire. 'I must say, this sounds most exciting.'

◆

I reached the racetrack early. I was dressed as a typical racegoer – camera and all – so as not to stand out, but this made it impossible for me to go to Bill's private office. Anyway, I didn't want to be seen with him.

Luckily, Bill had thought of a solution. I was approached by a cheeky-looking teenage girl who introduced herself as Carrie, one of Bill's daughters.

'Dad said you'd have a packet for him,' she said.

'And so I do,' I said. I gave it to her and that was that. I could now relax and enjoy the race.

It was a perfect afternoon. There were several good races, but the crowd of thousands was eagerly waiting for the main event. Only two horses from the train were running – Upper Gumtree and Flokati – although most of the owners, like the Lorrimores, had brought in other horses by road or air. So there was plenty of tension and excitement among the owners from the train.

As Mrs Baudelaire had said, the Lorrimores' Premiere led the field of twenty runners from the start, but to everyone's surprise Upper Gumtree made a late challenge and just beat Premiere at the post.

The owners, Mr and Mrs Unwin, were overjoyed. I was looking down from my seat on to the owners' area and watched everyone crowding around the Unwins and congratulating them. Only Filmer stood apart.

My eyes travelled carelessly from the owners over the rest of the crowd. I almost missed him! But yes, it was Thin-face. Before he could disappear in the crowd, I raised my camera and took his picture.

I immediately took the film out of the camera. I waited until most of the people had left the racetrack, and then it was easy to find Carrie again. She took the film to her father, who was by now carrying out one of the more enjoyable parts of his job – entertaining the winners.

Back at the hotel, I rang Mrs Baudelaire once again, to ask her to ask Bill to tell me as soon as possible who the man on the film was, if he could.

The train rolled out of Winnipeg that evening, and the celebrating went on late into the night, especially among the owners and the grooms.

At breakfast the next morning, however, the mood was completely different. For a start, Filmer stayed in his room; but the main problem was that Daffodil was clearly very angry. Sheridan's usual rudeness didn't help the atmosphere either.

34

Nell told me that Daffodil and Filmer had been heard having a row very late the night before; no one knew what it was about, but Daffodil was so upset that she was planning to leave the train at the next stop, which was Calgary.

Then George Burley called me into his office, where I found Leslie Brown waiting. 'Tell him what you told me,' George said to her.

'One of the grooms is behaving strangely,' she said.

'Which one?' I asked, although I had already guessed.

'The one who looks after Laurentide Ice,' said Ms Brown. 'I mean, all the grooms have headaches from drinking last night, but this one is sitting by himself in the horse-car; he's too quiet, as well as all white in the face.'

I went up to the horse-car with George. One look at the groom, whose name was Lenny Higgs, and I knew what was wrong: he was badly frightened.

It took time and patience, but I got the story out of him. Someone who sounded a lot like Thin-face had threatened to get him sent to prison for poisoning Mrs Quentin's other horse, Thunder. Thin-face had described prison to Lenny in detail, and Lenny was sure he would be beaten up and stabbed to death there.

'And did you poison the horse?' I asked.

'No, of course not!' protested Lenny. 'I loved old Thunder. But I gave him those sweets that Mrs Quentin said to give him.'

'Did you tell this man yesterday about the treats?'

'Yes, and that's when he said I'd go to prison. I don't want to go to prison, Mister. Can't you get me off this train?'

'Promise anything,' Catto always said, 'to keep them on your side.' So I promised I could protect him.

It took time and patience, but I got the story out of the groom. Someone who sounded a lot like Thin-face had threatened to get him sent to prison.

CHAPTER TEN

I had to act quickly. I left Lenny in George's hands and when the train arrived at Calgary, I rang Mrs Baudelaire on the radio phone and asked her to have Bill call me back immediately, from a private phone. I needed to speak to him directly and didn't know his number; in fact, I didn't even know whether he was still in Winnipeg or had returned to Toronto.

The phone rang within five minutes, and I told Bill about Lenny Higgs and Daffodil Quentin – about what he had said, and what she had not.

'What do you make of it?' he asked.

'It's fairly clear to me,' I said. 'Filmer's playing his usual games. He's using Thin-face – the man whose photograph I sent you – like he used Welfram in England, to frighten people. He frightened Higgs into telling him about Daffodil Quentin's "sweets" for her horse Thunder. Thin-face told Filmer, and Filmer is now threatening to report Mrs Quentin to the police or the Jockey Club or both unless she gives him the rest of Laurentide Ice. Mrs Quentin must know that the Jockey Club is already suspicious about the fact that three of her horses have died in such a short space of time, so she's scared – scared enough to feel that she has to give in to Filmer. And that makes her angry as well: no one likes to be threatened.'

'Hmm,' he said. 'I suppose you could be right. You know Filmer and his methods better than I do. What do you want me to do?'

'Collect Lenny from the station here and lay on another groom for Laurentide Ice,' I said. 'Offer Lenny a ticket to wherever in the world he wants to go to start a new life. Then, at the right time, we can tell Mrs Quentin that, without Lenny, Filmer's threats come to nothing. She won't have to give him the rest of Laurentide Ice, and we'll have stopped a criminal in one of his crimes. And that's at least part of my job. I know this won't be easy for you, since you are suspicious of Daffodil Quentin, and if she did poison her horses, you don't want to see her get away with it. I don't either, but stopping Filmer is more important than proving Daffodil guilty, don't you think?'

Bill thought for a short while and then said, 'I think I can live with myself if Mrs Quentin gets away with it. She may be stupid and greedy, but I don't think she's an absolute criminal like Filmer, do you?'

I agreed that she was not.

'And I think I can arrange everything you're asking me to arrange,' said Bill. 'I see why you had to ring me: I'm the only one who *could* arrange all that at short notice. But I'm glad we've spoken just now, otherwise I'd have had to wait to give you what is obviously important news.'

'What?' I asked excitedly.

'Val Catto says that the numbers are not a phone number, or anything to do with Filmer's birthday, or anything like that: they're his passport number. The numbers you want are 049. He also says that you are not to get arrested. Does this message make sense to you? It sounds odd to me. What are you doing?'

'Nothing you need to know about yet,' I said. I repeated the numbers to make sure I'd heard them correctly. Now all I had to do was wait for another chance to get into Filmer's room.

While Bill and I had been talking, through the window I watched Daffodil Quentin storm off the train and into a waiting taxi. Whatever had happened to the other three horses, she had certainly lost this one through evil means — and not her own, this time.

◆

The next stop was Lake Louise, high in the mountains, with the most breathtaking views of natural beauty I had ever seen. The hotel rooms all had huge windows so that one could constantly enjoy the sight of the brilliant blue lake, snow, mountains, pine trees, and the front of an advancing glacier – all against a background of further mountains in the distance.

Nell got everyone settled in their rooms and then joined me in the hotel lounge. I had decided to stay in the same hotel as the passengers, to keep an eye on things. Well, that's what I told Nell I was in the hotel for; in fact, I wanted another chance to look inside Filmer's briefcase. I was running a risk staying in the hotel, since this was not what a normal waiter would do, but the hotel was big enough for me to hide in.

'You'll have to eat alone in your room,' Nell observed.

'True.'

'You must lead a lonely life.'

'Also true.'

'Don't you mind?'

'Not usually,' I said. 'After all, it's my choice.'

'Not usually?' she asked, stressing the last word.

'Well, *you* could tempt me into a different way of life,' I said with a grin.

Nell said nothing in reply to that, but just looked at me.

'I mean, what are you doing after this trip?' I asked.

'Flying back to Toronto and my job, I suppose,' she said. 'Why? What did you have in mind?'

'How does two weeks in Hawaii sound?'

There was a pause, and then she said, 'I must go and look after the passengers.'

I caught her hand as she stood up. 'What about Hawaii?' I said.

'Don't you ever give up?' asked Nell.

'Not with you,' I said. 'Tell me you'll come to Hawaii.'

'I'll give you an answer in Vancouver,' she replied.

CHAPTER ELEVEN

In fact, no opportunities presented themselves at the hotel. It wasn't that Filmer stayed in his room most of the time, though he certainly didn't join in the expeditions the others organized between themselves. But even when he was out of his room, the door was securely locked, and I was not about to undertake a bit of breaking and entering. At breakfast, he brought his briefcase out of his room, and kept it close by him. The sight of it was a reminder of how close I was to discovering its secrets, if only I had the chance – and the courage. Of course, it may contain only perfectly innocent papers . . .

Nearly everyone went on an expedition the hotel had arranged in the morning. I stayed behind, of course, since waiters do not go on expeditions with wealthy horse-owners; Filmer stayed in his room; Xanthe Lorrimore wandered aimlessly around the hotel and its grounds looking bored and miserable. I doubted whether she even saw the scenery; I wondered whether she knew how much her parents needed her love, not her bad moods. They had enough trouble with Sheridan. Sheridan had real problems, but there was nothing wrong with Xanthe except the usual difficulties of being a teenager, combined with being immensely rich and spoiled.

The hotel lounge had magazines piled on coffee tables. In one of them I had read a saying of Mercer Lorrimore's: 'You're not better because you're richer, but you're richer because you're better.' I hoped that Xanthe would remember that.

Before leaving the hotel, I spoke to Mrs Baudelaire on the phone. She had no further news on Sheridan Lorrimore, but told me that the food I had sent to be analysed was harmless. So no one was trying to influence the Vancouver race in that way. Finally, she told me that Bill had not found anyone who recognized the thin-faced man in the photograph, but he was continuing to ask around. He'd also sent some copies of the photograph to me at the train: they should be there by now, she said.

When I reached the train, George handed me an envelope with the photographs in, which I put in my pocket. There was a great contrast between the cold outside and the warmth inside the train, and I was obviously appreciating the warmth.

'We're lucky to have heat on the train at the moment,' said George.

'Why?' I asked.

'They couldn't start the heater,' he said. He seemed to think it was a great joke, but I couldn't see the point.

'No fuel,' he explained.

I looked blank. 'So they had to get more oil,' I said.

'Of course,' George said, 'but they also filled up only two days ago. So the engineer had a look at the tank. But there were only a few drops left. Someone had opened the bottom tap and stolen the fuel.'

'You don't seem too worried,' I remarked.

'Well, no harm was done, was it? Anyway, this kind of thing happens all the time on the railways.'

'Was there a lot of oil on the ground?' I asked.

'You're not a bad detective,' George commented. 'Yes, there was. But that just means that whatever container the thief used overflowed on to the ground.'

'Does it?' I asked. 'Or does it mean that the tap was opened on purpose so that the oil would leak on to the ground? The tap was probably opened a while ago, and the oil has been leaking away during the train's journey, with only the last drops ending up on the ground here.'

'You've just got a suspicious mind,' said George.

'Yes,' I said, 'but now two unusual things have happened to this train. That may not seem odd to you, but it does to me.'

'You think this might have been sabotage as well?' asked George.

'I don't know,' I said, 'but it's not impossible, is it? And by the way, could you look at this?' I pulled the envelope out of my pocket, took one of the pictures out and showed it to him. 'This is the man I was asking you about earlier.'

'Yes, I have seen him,' he said, frowning slightly. 'Not on the train, though: it was on the platform yesterday. Of course, he might be travelling on the train: it's just that I haven't noticed him on it.'

'What was he doing on the platform yesterday?' I asked. 'Just standing there?'

'No,' said George. 'He was knocking on the door of the horse-car with a stick. You can imagine how pleased Leslie Brown was with that! She came and asked him what he wanted, and he said that he had a message for the groom of the grey horse. So Leslie went away and came back with the groom – only it wasn't the one your thin-faced man was expecting, was it? The new groom told your man that he had replaced the old groom in Calgary, and then your man in the photograph walked off. I didn't see where he went.'

'Did the man look angry or anything?' I asked.

'I didn't notice,' he said. He held out the photograph for me to take back, but I told him to keep it and I asked him to question the attendants from further up the train – if the man was a passenger, he must be among the racegoers.

'What's he done?' asked George. 'Anything yet?'

'Frightened a groom into leaving,' I said.

He stared. 'Not much of a crime.' His eyes laughed. 'He won't do much time in prison for that.'

CHAPTER TWELVE

On my way from George's office to the dining-car, to help Emil and the others, I met the sleeping-car attendant, with whom I had become friendly a couple of days before. A plan was starting to form in my mind.

We chatted for a few minutes about the scenery. He had never been this far west before, since he normally worked only on trains between Toronto and Winnipeg.

'What time do you turn the blankets down on the beds?' I asked.

'Any time after all the passengers have gone into the dining-car for the evening meal,' he said. 'Why?'

'I'll give you a hand with the beds, if you like.'

'You don't have to, you know.'

'I know, but I'd like to. It'll be a useful experience for me, if I want to work on trains.'

In the dining-car, I found the others hard at work, and apologized for being late again.

Soon the passengers started coming in and sitting at the tables. Night was falling fast over the mountains. Nell was sitting at a table with the Unwins, and they were complaining that the train would pass through the best scenery after dark. Nell said that she was sorry, but she didn't write the timetables; and she hoped that they had seen a mountain or two at Lake Louise.

Filmer came in trying to wipe a grin off his face. I didn't like the look of that: anything which made Filmer smile was certain to be bad news for someone else.

The Lorrimores sat together at one table: the children looked rebellious; Bambi looked bored; and Mercer looked as though his thoughts were elsewhere. I hoped that Filmer's good mood and Mercer's worry were not connected, although I was afraid that they might be.

I stayed long enough to serve the passengers their first glasses of champagne, and then explained to Emil that I would have to leave, but that I would be back before the meal was over. I didn't ask what he told Cathy, Oliver and the others about my mysterious behaviour. Perhaps he said nothing: they were nice people, and would take me on trust.

Once all the passengers were sitting and eating, I left the dining-car and went to find the sleeping-car attendant. 'Now?' I asked.

'Sure,' he said.

We went up to the door of the Youngs' room. The attendant knocked on the door. 'You must always knock,' he explained, 'even when you know they're not in.'

We entered and he showed me how to prepare the beds. 'That looks easy enough,' I said. 'You can leave me to do this end of the corridor, if you like, while you do the other end.'

'OK,' he said. 'Thanks.'

'Thank *you*,' I replied, and watched him walk off down the corridor.

The room next to the Youngs' was Filmer's. My heart was in my mouth as I knocked and entered. The briefcase was in the same place, under the bed. I pulled it out.

My hands were trembling as I turned the wheels on the lock: 049, and the left-hand lock opened; 151 for the right-hand one.

I was faced with a lot of boring papers about the Transcontinental Race Train — the brochure I'd already seen, Fulmer's ticket, and so on.

I was faced with a lot of boring papers about the Transcontinental Race Train – the brochure I'd already seen, Filmer's ticket, and so on. There was his passport, numbered H049151: good for the Brigadier.

The I came across a cutting from a newspaper – a newspaper from Cambridge, England. It said that one of the colleges had been given a large amount of money by the famous Canadian banker Mercer P. Lorrimore, to go towards building a new library. My God! What was Filmer doing with that?

Underneath the cutting was another piece of paper. It was completely blank apart from a short typewritten report. There were no marks to betray where it had come from, but it mentioned the horrible ways in which seven cats had been killed in 'the College' – it didn't say which college. Most of the cats had had their heads cut off, or worse; all of them had been treated with extreme cruelty before being killed.

I nearly had a heart attack when I heard a knock at the door. But it was only the sleeping-car attendant. He had wondered why I was taking so long. 'Can I help?' he asked.

'No,' I said. 'I'm just coming.'

I took one last look at the cutting and the report, so that I would remember the details, pushed the briefcase back under the bed and left the room.

'I had some trouble,' I explained to the attendant. 'It's not as easy as it looks to get everything perfectly neat and tidy.'

'Are you all right?' he asked. 'You look all hot.'

'I'll be OK now,' I said. 'Thanks.'

At that moment, Filmer himself came from the dining-car. 'Hey, you!' he said to me. 'Were you in my bedroom?'

'Yes, sir,' I said. 'I was making your bed ready for the night, sir.'

'Oh,' he said, accepting what I'd said. He went into his room.

I waited outside in the corridor, expecting him to storm out of his room any second and accuse me of going through his belongings. But nothing happened and I breathed freely again.

CHAPTER THIRTEEN

The food that night was particularly good. It was our last night on the train, and Angus was determined to make it special. Judging by the looks on people's faces, he had succeeded. I only hoped that some of the food would be left over, for a poor starving waiter to enjoy. But it didn't seem as though any would be.

I was kept busy serving champagne. Mercer even allowed Sheridan some; but Mercer was still clearly not in the party mood, and Sheridan was looking blank, as if he had stopped thinking, or was thinking very deeply. I was pleased, however, to see that Xanthe was trying hard to get her father to enjoy himself. When the meal was over and the passengers demanded that Angus be brought from the kitchen, so that they could congratulate him, Xanthe was among the first to clap as he bowed awkwardly. The snow falling in the mountains outside added to the party atmosphere.

Nell was standing at the end of the dining-car, watching Angus, and I managed to position myself next to her.

'Xanthe wants to have a good time,' I whispered. 'Couldn't you rescue her from the rest of her family?'

'What's the matter with them?' Nell asked.

'Xanthe might tell you, if she knows,' I said.

Nell flashed me an observant glance. 'And if she tells me, you want me to tell you, I suppose.'

'Yes, please, since you ask.'

'One day you'll have to explain all this to me.'

'One day soon,' I promised.

I went back to the kitchen to help with washing the dishes and to find something to eat. As I'd thought, there wasn't much. Afterwards, I started preparing the tables for breakfast the next morning. While I was doing that, Nell came in and sat down at the table I was laying.

'For what it's worth,' she said, 'Xanthe doesn't know why her parents are so upset. She says it can't have been something Mr Filmer said to them just before dinner, because that sounded so silly.'

'Did she tell you what he said?' I asked.

Nell nodded. 'Xanthe said Mr Filmer asked her father if he would let him have Voting Right, and her father said he wouldn't part with the horse for anything. They were both still smiling and friendly, Xanthe said. It was just small talk, it seemed. Then Mr Filmer, still smiling, said, "We'll have to have a little talk about cats." And that was all. Mr Filmer went into the dining-car. Xanthe asked her father what Mr Filmer had meant, and he said, "Don't bother me, darling."' Nell shook her head in puzzlement. 'So anyway, Xanthe is now having a good time in the bar and the rest of the Lorrimores have returned to their own car, and I'm exhausted, if you want to know.'

'Go to bed, then,' I suggested.

'One of your better ideas,' she said. 'You've got a strange look in your eyes, though, as if you're planning something. What is it?'

'I haven't done a thing,' I said.

'I'm not so sure,' Nell said. She stood up and went off to bed. I knew that I didn't want to lose her. I had known her only a week, and my mind said that was not long enough, but my heart was already certain.

I walked up the train to talk to George Burley; he was in his office as usual. 'I showed that photograph around,' he said. 'Is that what you came to see me about?'

'Yes.'

'He's definitely on the train. His name's Johnson, according to the passenger list. He stays in his room most of the time, the attendant up there tells me, and never talks to anyone, except one of the owners who goes up to see him sometimes.'

'Really?' I said. 'How interesting.'

'It gets more interesting,' said George. 'The owner was up there earlier this evening, and it seems he and Johnson had a row.'

'Did your assistant hear what it was about?'

'Important, is it?'

'Yes, it could be very important.'

'Well, no, he didn't hear exactly. He said he thought the owner was telling Johnson not to do something Johnson wanted to do. At any rate, when the owner left, Johnson called after him, "You can't stop me doing what I like."'

'That's not much help,' I said, 'since we don't know what he likes to do – except that he can be violent.'

'I know,' said George, 'but I've got one more thing to tell you. My assistant has worked on the railway for over thirty years; he says he recognizes Johnson from before. Johnson used to be a railwayman, but he was sacked and now hates the rail company.'

'And he could know how to unhitch the Lorrimores' car,' I exclaimed.

'Exactly,' said George.

'But now we've got two people to worry about. Johnson must have told Filmer that the groom, Lenny, has gone, so Filmer knows that Daffodil Quentin is out of his reach. What will Filmer do next, and what will Johnson do next, now that he is threatening to act separately from Filmer? Do you think you could ask your assistant to travel in the horse-car with Leslie, just to be on the safe side?'

'OK,' said George. 'No problem.' He set off immediately to see to it.

CHAPTER FOURTEEN

Back in my room, I lay down with all my clothes on, meaning just to rest – and immediately fell fast asleep. But I was woken up only half an hour later by someone calling for George. The first thing I realized was that the train had stopped, and that set off alarm bells in my mind, since we were not due to stop for another two hours, in Kamloops.

I went out into the corridor and found George's aged assistant – the one who was travelling with Leslie Brown in the horse-car.

'Where's George?' he asked.

'I don't know,' I said. 'What's the matter?'

'We've got a hot box,' he said, as if that explained everything. He seemed very worried by it, whatever it was.

'What's a hot box?' I asked.

'An overheated **axle**,' he said. 'But don't worry about the details. Let's just find George. He must radio Kamloops to get them to stop the Canadian. It must be only a few miles behind us, I'd guess.'

'I can use the radio,' I said. 'Come on.'

When we reached George's office, however, I saw that no one could use the radio. There was an empty coffee cup beside it and it was wet: someone had poured George's coffee on it. And the radio phone wouldn't work out here

50

in the middle of nowhere. There was still no sign of George.

'How long will it take for the axle to cool down?' I asked. I was now beginning to get thoroughly alarmed.

'Quite a while. It's red-hot at the moment. The engineers are putting snow on it, but it'll take longer to cool it down than the Canadian will take to reach here.'

'There must be something we can do. What did you used to do in the old days, before radios were invented?'

'Plant **flares**.'

'What do you mean?'

'Someone has to walk back along the track and plant flares by the side of the track and light them so that the Canadian will see them and stop . . . I'm too old – you'll have to go.'

He opened a cupboard in George's office and took out three objects which looked like large matches, with sharp ends for sticking into the ground.

'You can light them on a rail or a rock,' he explained. 'They burn bright red, for twenty minutes. You'll have to go at least half a mile back down the track, because the Canadian takes that long to stop once it has started to brake. And then walk back towards us with the third flare.'

'Why?'

'Because if the driver doesn't see the first two, you'll have to throw the third one in through the window of the engine: the window's always open because of the heat.'

I stared at him. 'That sounds impossible.'

'But that's what you've got to do. The train will be going at only about 35 m.p.h.* But don't worry: I'm sure the driver will see the first two flares. Go on now. Hurry.' He suddenly grabbed another flare from the cupboard. 'You'd better take another one, just in case.'

---

* Miles per hour, a measure of speed.

'In case of what?' What else could there be?

'In case of wild animals.'

◆

I set off east past the end of the train, along the single railway track. One arm held the four flares, while the other hand grasped a torch.

Half a mile. How long was half a mile?

Hurry, George's assistant had said. That was hardly a necessary instruction ... I half walked, half ran along the centre of the track. It had stopped snowing, but it was bitterly cold. My efforts and my fear would keep me warm, I thought – or at least keep me from noticing the cold.

I didn't see the danger in time. It moved fast, but at least I could tell that it was human, not an animal. He must have been hiding behind rocks or trees at the edge of the track. I sensed, rather than saw, a raised arm, a blow coming.

The Brigadier's saying, 'Thought before action', did not apply here: there was less than a second for purely instinctive action. I bent forward at the last moment, so that the blow landed across my shoulders, not on my head.

The pain was terrible. I fell to one knee, dropping the torch and the flares. I knew there was another blow on the way. I turned to face my attacker, so that I was inside and under his descending arm. I pushed myself upwards to crash into his chin with my head, and at the same time raised my knee violently between his legs. One of the many things I had learned during my years of rough travelling throughout the world was how to fight dirty – I had never needed the knowledge more than I did now.

He cried out in pain and fell to the ground; as he did so I grabbed the heavy piece of wood from his hands and hit him on the head with it. I hoped I had hit him hard enough to knock him out, but not enough to kill him. He lay face down in the snow by the rails. I turned him over with my foot, picked up the torch and saw the thin face of Johnson.

CHAPTER FIFTEEN

The pain in my back was increasing. I hoped that nothing was broken, but it felt awful. The effort of fighting had scarcely helped the pain.

I looked for the flares, but could find only three of them. I decided not to waste time hunting for the fourth, and just hoped any wild animals would stay well away.

It was very difficult to concentrate on anything. I had to get moving – acting rather than thinking. I certainly hadn't yet done half a mile. But how far had I come? I couldn't see the rear of the train, which was round a bend I hadn't noticed taking. And now, because of all the fighting and the walking around hunting for flares, I didn't know which way to go; the rocks and the trees looked the same in both directions. For a moment, I was afraid I would set out in the wrong direction. I forced myself to think – which was not easy because of all the pain. Yes, the wind had been in my face . . . and there were my footprints in the snow.

I set off again. How long did it take to walk half a mile in the snow on railway tracks? How much further should I go to be safe? In my mind, the rails seemed to go on and on for ever.

Johnson had been waiting for me – or for whoever would come from the train. That meant he knew that the radio couldn't be used, so he was the one who had sabotaged it. I began to feel even more worried about George being missing; and I began to think that the overheated axle had also been caused by Johnson – more sabotage. He wanted revenge on the railways; Filmer had used him, but had now lost control of him. Johnson had wanted to sit in the forest and watch one train crash into another. This is the typical behaviour of that kind of criminal: they like to watch the death and destruction their actions cause. I was determined that his plan would not succeed: there would be no crash.

By now I must have gone over half a mile, surely. I stopped and looked at my watch. The Canadian was due very soon. There was another curve ahead: if I just went around that, the driver would have more time to see the flares.

I must succeed. I ran around the final curve, put the torch down beside the track, and tried to light one of the flares on the rail. I scratched it again and again on the rail, begging it out loud to light. At last it lit, with a huge red rush which took me by surprise. I nearly dropped the flare. I pushed its sharp end into the ground by the track. It burned so brightly that the driver of the Canadian couldn't fail to see it – or so I hoped.

I ran further back up the track, around the next bend. Past this bend the track ran straight for a good long way: this was an even better place to plant a flare. I lit another one and stuck it in the ground.

Then I saw pin-sized lights in the distance. At first I thought they were the lights of houses, but then I saw that they were growing all the time. It was the Canadian, advancing fast . . . and it wasn't stopping! There was no urgent scream of brakes. But he *must* have seen the flare.

In slow motion, it seemed, I lit the last flare and got ready to throw it through the driver's window. As the train approached, it appeared huge and I appeared tiny. The window was so small and so high off the ground. I could see no faces in it – the driver and his assistant must be elsewhere.

I threw the flare — threw it too soon, missed the empty black window. It rolled off the engine and away down the other side.

'Stop!' I shouted, or perhaps prayed. I threw the flare – threw it high, threw it too soon, missed the empty black window. It rolled off the engine and away down the other side. The Canadian went on its mindless way around the curve and out of sight.

I felt sick; I had failed. People would die because I had failed. The pain of my back, which I had forgotten for a short time, suddenly returned. I picked up the torch and started to walk back the way I had come – and the way the Canadian had gone.

I imagined the scene, the Canadian driving at full speed into the Race Train, the broken wood and twisted metal, the bodies . . . Surely someone must have warned the Lorrimores and got them out of the rear car. I prayed that Nell would be safe. The thought of Nell made me speed up into a run. There, beside the track, was the useless flare I had thrown at the window, still burning red as if to blame me for failing, for betraying my job and my Nell.

I ran as fast as I could around the bend, listening for any sounds. My feet felt heavy, so that I seemed not to be moving, like in a dream.

There was nothing – no noise except the wind and my feet on the snow. I wondered when I would hear the crash of metal tearing into metal. It wasn't just the mountain air that was making me feel cold.

There were two red lights on the rails far ahead. They weren't bright and burning, like the flares; they were small and dim. I wondered what they were; my frozen mind wasn't working. Then I realized that they were the rear lights of a train . . . a train . . . it could only be one train . . . there had been no crash . . . no tragedy . . . The Canadian had *stopped*! Relief washed over me and I felt near to tears. The Canadian had stopped.

CHAPTER SIXTEEN

I ran towards the lights. Soon I began to see the outline of the train. I was suddenly afraid that it would start up again – this was not a reasonable thought, but fear is not reasonable.

I reached the train and now I was running along its side. There were people on the ground by the engine. They could see someone running towards them with a torch, and when I was fairly near to them, one of them shouted out, 'Get back on the train! There's no need for people to be out here!'

I slowed to a walk, very out of breath. 'No,' I said, 'I'm . . . I'm not from this train. I'm from the one in front.' I pointed up ahead, but the lights of the Canadian showed nothing except trees and snow and tracks.

'What train?' one of them said.

'The Transcontinental Race Train,' I gasped. 'It's up there. You can't see it, because it's around the corner.'

'But the Race Train is supposed to be thirty-five minutes ahead of us,' said the engineer.

'It had a hot box,' I said, although this meant little to me.

'Oh, I see,' said the engineer. He and the conductor decided to start the Canadian moving forward very slowly. I was glad not to have to walk any more, and I had a chance to recover my breath.

When we were all inside, and the engineer had released the brake, he asked me, 'How far ahead is the other train?'

'I don't know exactly. I can't remember how far I ran.'

'Was it you who lit the flares?'

'Yes.'

'Did you *throw* one of them?'

'Yes, I had to. I thought you hadn't seen the others. I didn't think you were going to stop.'

'It was just as well you did throw that last one,' said the

driver. 'I had bent down to pick up a tool. I didn't see the flare you threw, but I heard the noise of it hitting the engine, and I stood up just in time to see another one by the side of the track. Rather lucky.'

That was an understatement, if I'd ever heard one.

'Why didn't your conductor use his radio?' asked the conductor of the Canadian.

'The radio's out of order,' I explained.

There was a bend up ahead. 'I think we're close now,' I said. 'Please be careful.'

'Right,' said the engineer. He drove around the bend as slowly as possible – and braked to a stop about twenty yards from the end of the Lorrimores' carriage.

'Well,' said the driver drily, 'I wouldn't want to come around the corner at 35 m.p.h. and be faced with that.'

We climbed down from the engine and went to meet the crew from the Race Train. It was as if they knew that the Canadian would stop: they didn't talk about flares and accidents, they talked about hot boxes. It turned out that the oil had leaked away from one of the axle boxes on the horse-car, causing the axle to overheat. They were still applying snow, and thought they could refill the box with oil and get the train started again in about ten minutes.

No one had been able to find George Burley yet. George's assistant said it was a good thing that he had been travelling in the horse-car: he had recognized the smell of the overheating box and raised the alarm. If he hadn't, the axle would have broken, the train would have come off the rails, and a very serious accident would have happened.

'Did you warn any of the passengers?' I asked.

'No,' said the assistant. 'There was no need to wake them up.'

I couldn't believe my ears. 'But the Canadian might not have stopped.'

'Of course it would, when it saw the flares.'

Their trust amazed me and frightened me. The conductor of the Canadian said that he would radio ahead to Kamloops; both trains would have to stop again there. People in Kamloops would soon be getting worried, he said, about the failure of the Race Train to arrive.

For the first time, I remembered Johnson lying back there in the snow. I hadn't seen him on the way back, and wondered whether he had woken up and run away. I didn't particularly care what had happened to him, but thinking about him made me realize where George must be.

'Johnson's room,' I told the assistant. 'Look in there for George.'

'I can't go knocking on passengers' doors in the middle of the night,' protested the assistant.

'If Johnson's in there,' I said, 'I'll apologize to him myself.'

Johnson wasn't in there, of course, but George was. He was tied up, and had a cloth, fixed down with sticky tape, filling his mouth so that he couldn't cry out. He had been twisting and turning, but had not been able to escape. He had also been hit on the head – perhaps with the same piece of wood that had been used on me. I pulled the tape off his mouth.

'Ouch, that hurt,' complained George, but the look in his eyes showed that he was feeling more pleasure than pain.

CHAPTER SEVENTEEN

George sat in his office, drinking hot tea and refusing to lie down. He was refusing to admit that the blow on the head which had knocked him out was having any effect on him now. As soon as he was free of the ropes and had been told about the hot box, he insisted on a meeting between himself, the conductor of the Canadian, myself and other staff members from both trains. Together with the radioman in Kamloops, they agreed that the Race Train would set off as soon as possible, with the Canadian about ten minutes behind. In Kamloops the order would be reversed, with the Canadian going first, while the Race Train remained in Kamloops for a few hours for all the axle boxes to be checked. There would be no official investigation in Kamloops, since it was the middle of the night: the investigation could wait until Vancouver. Everyone nodded in agreement with this plan: George looked white, as if he wished he hadn't moved his head.

The crew soon had the axle cool enough and they refilled the box with oil. The Canadian's crew returned to their train, and the Race Train set off once again. I was sitting with George in his office. He demanded to know everything that had happened, from start to finish.

'First, you tell me how you came to be knocked out,' I said.

'I can't remember. I was walking up to see the engineers.' He looked puzzled. 'Then I was lying there all tied up. I was there for ages. It was Johnson's room, they tell me, so I suppose it was Johnson who did it. Where is he now?'

I told George about Johnson's attacking me and how I'd left him, but hadn't seen him on the way back.

'There are two possibilities,' George said, 'or three, I suppose. Either he's left, or he's getting a ride on the Canadian right at this moment.'

I stared; I hadn't thought of that. 'What's the third possibility?'

'The wild animals out on the mountain,' George said, not unhappily.

Before long we ran into Kamloops, where all the axles were checked, the radio replaced, and everything else went according to plan. Once we were moving again, George finally agreed to lie down and try to sleep, and I was only too glad to do the same.

Things always start hurting when one has time to think about them. The dull pain in my left shoulder where Johnson had hit me was worse and sharper when I lay down. I won't make a very good waiter in the morning, I thought, with a stiff shoulder.

I smiled to myself finally. In spite of Filmer's and Johnson's best efforts, the Transcontinental Race Train might yet limp into Vancouver without disaster.

I should have remembered the saying about not counting chickens.

◆

The pain in my shoulder forced me out of bed after only a few hours, and I was in time to help the others prepare for breakfast. While we were doing so, the train stopped for quarter of an hour in a place called North Bend, which was our last stop before Vancouver. From here on, the train ran down the Fraser **Canyon** into Vancouver.

As we travelled through the Fraser Canyon, from the left side of the train I could look almost straight down to the huge river far below, rushing white between walls of stone. The railway track seemed to be hanging over the edge.

I was taking a basket of bread down to the end of the dining-car when Mercer Lorrimore came in. He asked if I could bring hot tea through to his own car.

'Certainly, sir,' I said. 'Anything else?'

'No, just tea for the three of us.'

When I took it along there, I found Sheridan almost lying in an easy chair, with the same blank look on his face that he'd worn the night before. All I could think of was cats.

His father asked me politely to put the tray down on the table and to come back in half an hour for it.

Nell and Xanthe had arrived in the dining-car during my absence. Nell frowned at my appearance: I suppose some of the pain was showing on my face.

'Have you heard that we are running an hour and a half late, madam?' I said, in proper waiter fashion, as I offered her the menu.

'No,' she said, and looked up at me with a question in her eyes.

'We had to stop in Kamloops to get the radio fixed,' I said by way of explanation. She would be telling the passengers the reason for the delay, and that was all they needed to know.

Others had noticed the train stopping in the night, but everyone was content to accept my story. I was tempted to say to Filmer, 'Actually, the real reason is that your man Johnson nearly succeeded in wrecking the train – and probably killing you along with everyone else.'

After half an hour, I went along to the Lorrimores' car to collect the tray of tea things. I knocked, but as there was no answer I entered anyway.

Mercer was standing there in shock.

'Sir?' I said.

'My son,' he said.

Sheridan wasn't in the room. Mercer was alone.

'Stop the train,' he said. 'We must go back.'

Oh *God*, I thought.

'He went to the back . . . to look at the river from the balcony . . .' Mercer could hardly speak. 'When I looked up, he wasn't there.'

CHAPTER EIGHTEEN

I went over to the balcony. The door between the balcony and the carriage was closed; the balcony was empty. It looked down on to the angry river, hundreds of feet below in the canyon. Death was there – a quick death.

I went back into the carriage and closed the door.

'Sit down, sir,' I said, taking his arm. 'I'll tell the conductor. He'll know what to do.'

'We must go back.' He sat down heavily on the chair. 'He went out . . . and when I looked . . .'

'Will you be all right while I fetch the conductor?'

He nodded dully.

I hurried down to George's room, ignoring everyone in the dining-car, and knocked on the door. There was no reply. I knocked harder and called his name. There was a sound from inside. I opened the door and found him waking from a deep sleep.

I closed the door, sat on the edge of his bed and told him we'd lost a passenger.

'What? Who?'

'Sheridan Lorrimore.'

'When? Where?'

'About ten minutes ago, I should think, into the Fraser Canyon.'

He swore violently and stretched out a hand for the radio, looking out of the window. 'It's no use going back, you know. Not if he went into the water from this high up. He'd have hit rocks on the way down and the water in the river is bitterly cold, even if he was alive when he reached the bottom of the canyon.'

'His father will want to go back, though.'

'Of course.'

He started talking to a radioman in Vancouver. He explained that Mercer Lorrimore's son – yes, *the* Mercer Lorrimore – had fallen from the rear of the train into the Fraser Canyon. Lorrimore wanted the train stopped so that he could go back and try to find his son.

'I think I'd better go back to Mercer,' I said.

George nodded. 'Tell him I'll come to talk to him when I get instructions from my head office.'

As I passed through the dining-car, I paused by Nell's and Xanthe's table and whispered to Nell to bring Xanthe to the private carriage. Nell looked inquiringly into my face, but they got up and followed me.

As we entered the Lorrimores' car, Mercer came out of his and Bambi's bedroom. Bambi could be heard crying; Mercer's face was grey and hollow-eyed.

'Daddy!' Xanthe cried, pushing past me. 'What's the matter?'

He took her in his arms and quietly told her about Sheridan. We were unable to hear his words, but we heard her say, 'No! He couldn't have!'

'Who couldn't have done what?' Nell asked me.

'Sheridan went off the balcony into the canyon.'

'Do you mean . . . ? Is he dead?'

'I would think so.'

Mercer said, 'Why aren't we stopping? We have to go back.' But he no longer sounded as though he expected Sheridan to be alive.

'The conductor is on the radio now, sir,' I said, 'getting instructions.'

He nodded. He was a reasonable man. He only had to look out of the window to see that there was no hope of finding his son alive. He also knew that it was impossible for anyone to fall off that balcony by accident: Sheridan had jumped.

He took her in his arms and quietly told her about Sheridan. We were unable to hear his words, but we heard her say, 'No! He couldn't have.'

Mercer sat on the sofa, his arm around Xanthe. Xanthe wasn't crying: she looked serious and calm. The tragedy hadn't happened for her within that half hour, it had been happening all her life. Her brother had been lost to her even when he was alive.

CHAPTER NINETEEN

Nell asked Mercer whether she could do anything for Mrs Lorrimore, or whether she and I should go.

'No,' Mercer said, 'but please stay in case she needs you.'

At that moment, George arrived. He started by telling Mercer how sorry he was about the accident.

'We have to go back,' Mercer said.

'Yes, sir, but not the whole train, sir. My instructions are that the train must go on to Vancouver as planned.'

Mercer began to protest, but George interrupted him. 'Sir, my head office has already informed all the authorities along the canyon to look out for your son. They also say that they will arrange transport for you and your family to return, as soon as we reach Vancouver. From there, you can go to a small town at the south end of the canyon; the town is called . . . er . . . Hope. And then you'll be in the area if there is any news of your son.'

'So how soon could we be in Hope?' Mercer asked.

'If you leave Vancouver at four this afternoon, you'll be there by seven.'

'That's useless,' Mercer said. 'I'll get a helicopter.'

There was absolutely no point in being rich, I thought, if one didn't know how to use it.

Nell said she would get her travel company to lay on a car to meet the Lorrimores at Vancouver station, and arrange for the helicopter. George, Nell and I got up to leave. I picked up the tea tray and asked if there was anything I could bring them, but Mercer shook his head.

'I'll come and find you,' Xanthe said, 'if they need anything.' She sounded grown up, years older than she was at breakfast.

Once we'd left the room, George explained to Nell that she would have to wait until we were closer to Vancouver before making a phone call to her travel company, because the phone would not work until then. Then he hurried off.

Nell sighed and wondered what to tell the other passengers. 'It'll spoil the end of their trip,' she said.

But I had a different view of human nature. 'I bet you that they express sympathy for about ten seconds,' I said, 'and then go around saying "Isn't it awful?" for the rest of the morning, but without it spoiling anything for them.'

I was right.

However, Julius Apollo Filmer was no longer in the dining-car, which was a pity – I would have liked to have seen his face when he heard the news. Sheridan Lorrimore was Filmer's lever against his father. What would he do now? He could either give up trying to threaten Mercer Lorrimore, or he might still think that Mercer would want to protect his son's memory, and would sacrifice a horse for that.

◆

I helped to clear away breakfast, wash the dishes and pack everything away in boxes; then that was the end of my duties as a waiter. I felt that I had not been a very good one: apart from anything else, I had sometimes been busy elsewhere when the others were hard at work. Nevertheless, Emil and his crew thanked me and insisted on sharing the tips they had received with me. I was very touched by their kindness.

'We know you're not a waiter,' said Emil, 'but you have worked for it. It's yours.'

'And this morning,' added Cathy, 'you've worked despite obviously having a sore arm.'

We said our goodbyes, and I knew that I would never again curse a waiter, now that I knew how hard his job was.

I decided that I still wouldn't tell the passengers who I really was, until the game was finally over. I would continue to be the invisible man – only a waiter.

The passengers were busy packing their cases and having little parties in one another's rooms. I passed by Nell's room and found her packing too.

'What's wrong with your arm?' she asked as she folded a skirt.

'Is it so obvious?'

'To anyone looking at you, yes,' she said.

'It's not serious.'

'I don't believe you. I'll find you a doctor in Vancouver.'

'Don't be silly,' I said, though I was glad she cared.

George came and told Nell that we were now close enough to Vancouver for the phone to work. I accompanied her down to George's office while she made her call. She came out of the office very quickly.

'There's no need for the helicopter,' she announced. 'Sheridan has already been found.'

'Dead?' I asked.

'Very.'

'You'd better tell Mercer.'

She wasn't happy about that idea. 'You do it.'

'I can't – not as a waiter. George could, I suppose.'

George agreed to take the news to the Lorrimores, and went off immediately to do so.

Nell was starting to relax now that the trip was ending,

and apart from my shoulder I was starting to feel happier too. I told Nell so, and then joked that my boss was always threatening to sack me for being too happy.

'I can never tell when you're being serious,' said Nell. 'Who is your boss, anyway?'

'Brigadier Valentine Catto,' I replied, and then, 'I've just had a brilliant idea.'

'Yes, you rather look like it.'

'You don't happen to have a world air timetable with you, do you?'

'Yes, of course. What do you want? Are you planning to leave suddenly?'

'No, but you could tell me the times of flights from London to Vancouver tomorrow.'

CHAPTER TWENTY

The passengers were all leaving for their hotel; I looked at the hotel list to make sure that Filmer was on it. He was bound to stay on in Vancouver for the races, but I wanted to be certain. I also persuaded George to remain in Vancouver for a couple of days, before he returned to Toronto. All I had to do was tell him my plan, and he readily agreed to stay.

I went to my hotel – not the same one as Filmer and his fellow passengers – and telephoned to England. I found the Brigadier at his club.

'Tor!' he said. 'Where are you?' I could hear murmurs in the background and imagined the dark oak walls, the antique furniture and the pictures of famous sportsmen and former club members.

'Vancouver,' I replied. 'Can I phone you again soon when you're alone? This is going to take some time to explain.'

'Is it urgent?'

'Yes.'

'I'll have them transfer this call up to my bedroom. Just wait a couple of minutes.'

So before long, I had explained my plan to him.

'I won't say it's impossible,' he said when I had finished, 'but it's certainly not going to be easy.'

'There's a flight out of London airport tomorrow at three in the afternoon,' I replied, 'which should give you plenty of time – with a bit of luck.'

'What does Bill Baudelaire say?'

'I haven't asked him yet; I'll be ringing him next. I wanted your reaction first.'

'I'll ring you back in ten minutes, when I've had time to think it over,' Catto said. 'What's your phone number?'

'Thought before action?' I asked.

'It's always best, if there's time,' he replied.

I gave him the phone number and waited. In fact, it was twenty minutes before he rang back – twenty nervous minutes for me.

'All right,' he said. 'If Baudelaire approves, so do I. And, of course, if we can't find the information you need in the available time, then we cannot proceed with this plan. And apart from that, Tor, well done.'

◆

I was looking forward to speaking to Mrs Baudelaire again. I dialled her number and Bill himself answered.

'Hello,' I said, surprised. 'It's Tor Kelsey. How's your mother?'

There was a long pause. 'She . . . er . . . died early this morning.'

I didn't know what to say. I realized how fond I had

become of her. 'I can't believe it,' I said. 'I spoke to her only recently.'

'We knew, and she knew, that at the most it would only be weeks,' Bill said. 'And then yesterday evening there was a crisis.'

I was silent. I had wanted so much to meet her when all this was over. 'Your mother was great,' I said. 'I'm so sorry.'

'She thought the same about you.' Bill's voice got stronger. 'And Tor, she would have wanted us to go on. She loved horse-racing, and hated people like Filmer who tried to make it dirty. We would both fail her if we didn't go straight on. I've had hours to think this out. The last thing she would want would be for us to give up. So, we've had a letter from Filmer announcing that Laurentide Ice now belongs entirely to him, but we're going to inform him that the Canadian Jockey Club is removing his licence to own horses in Canada.'

'Er . . . I'd like to do it differently,' I said.

'How do you mean?'

I sighed deeply and talked to him too for a long time. He listened as the Brigadier had, and at the end said simply, 'I do wish she'd been alive to hear all this.'

'Yes, so do I.'

'Well,' he said, 'I'll go along with it. The real problem is time. You'd better talk to Mercer Lorrimore yourself.'

'But . . .'

'No buts. You're there. I'm not. Talk to him straight away, otherwise he might just collect Sheridan's body and return to Toronto.'

'Yes, you're right.'

'Of course. Use all the authority you need. The Brigadier and I will support you.'

◆

71

As soon as I'd finished speaking to Bill, I rang Mercer at his hotel, but it was Nell who answered the phone.

'Bambi doesn't want to speak to anyone at the moment,' she explained, 'and Mercer and Xanthe have gone to Hope to collect Sheridan's body. So all their phone calls are being sent to my room.'

'When will Mercer and Xanthe be back, do you know?'

'About six.'

'You see, the Jockey Club asked me to set up a meeting. Could you tell Mercer that when he gets back to his hotel, a car will be waiting to bring him to a brief meeting with the Jockey Club?'

'Yes, I guess I could,' she said. 'Do you want Xanthe too?'

'No, definitely not. Mercer alone.'

'Is it important? He's got enough troubles at the moment.'

'Yes, I think it is important – important for him,' I said.

CHAPTER TWENTY-ONE

So that evening the car I had ordered brought Mercer Lorrimore to my hotel for a meeting. The driver told him which room to go up to. He knocked on the door and I let him in.

He took about two steps into the room and stopped when he recognized me.

'What is this?' he said angrily.

He seemed ready to leave, so I closed the door behind him.

'I work for the British Jockey Club,' I said. 'I was sent here to work with the Canadian Jockey Club during the Race Train journey.'

'But you're . . . you're a waiter!'

'My name is Tor Kelsey,' I said. 'We thought it better if I didn't go openly on the train as a sort of policeman for the Jockey Club, so I went as a waiter.'

'My God,' he said weakly. He stepped further into the room. 'Why am I here? What do you want?'

'I believe you know both Bill Baudelaire and Brigadier Valentine Catto?'

He nodded.

'As they cannot be here, they have both given me permission to speak to you for them.'

'Yes, but about what?'

I showed him a chair. 'Would you like to sit down? And would you like a drink?'

He nearly smiled at the echo of my act as a waiter, but he sat down. He asked to see my passport to prove that I was who I was claiming to be. The passport gave my occupation as investigator.

He handed it back. 'Yes, I'll have a drink,' he said, 'as you're so good at serving them.' I served him his drink, as I had done so many times on the train. Then he said. 'No one on the train guessed about you. Why were you there, though?'

'I was sent because of one of the passengers. Because of Julius Filmer.'

He had been beginning to relax, but my statement made him tense again. He put the glass down on the table beside him and stared at me.

'Mr Lorrimore,' I said, sitting down opposite him, 'I am sorry about your son. And all the members of the Jockey Club send their sympathy. But I think you should know straight away that Brigadier Catto, Bill Baudelaire and myself know all about the ... er ... the cats at Sheridan's college in Cambridge.'

He looked deeply shocked. 'You can't know!'

'Don't worry, it's not public knowledge. I found out, and I had to tell Catto and Baudelaire. But Filmer knows too, doesn't he?'

He made a helpless gesture with his hands. 'Yes, but I don't understand how he could have found out.'

'We're working on that very question,' I said.

'Sheridan knew,' Mercer said. 'I mean he knew I was worried, and he heard Filmer's nasty little remark about the cats, and whatever else Sheridan was, he was not stupid: he could add two and two. And that last evening, he was different – he seemed to be thinking something over.'

I nodded and said that I'd noticed.

'And then that morning,' Mercer continued, 'he said, "Sorry, Dad", just before he went out to the balcony. I asked him what he meant, and he said, "I made a real mess of things for you, didn't I?" We all knew he had, but it was the first time he had admitted it; and I didn't guess that he was talking specially about the situation with Filmer and Voting Right and the cats. You know what Filmer wanted, do you?'

I nodded.

'It wasn't the only time Sheridan had killed cats, you know,' Mercer went on. 'He killed two cats like that when he was fourteen, in our garden. A doctor said that it was just a phase and would pass . . . It never did, but we hoped he would be all right at Cambridge. Instead, he got worse . . . I'll never know if he intended to jump into the canyon, or if it was a sudden idea of his . . .' Mercer looked me in the eyes and made a simple statement: 'I loved my son.'

He stopped talking. I let him sit and drink in silence for a while. Eventually, a sigh showed that his thoughts were turning away from Sheridan. Then it was my turn, and not for the first time that day I talked for a long time about what I planned to do.

By the time I was half-way through, I knew that he would do what I was asking, and I was grateful, because it wouldn't be easy for him.

He sat in his chair, nodding in agreement with everything I was saying – with both the action and the thought behind the action. When I'd finished, he said, still surprised, 'The waiter . . .'

'I'd be grateful,' I said, 'if you don't tell anyone else about my disguise.'

'I won't,' he promised.

CHAPTER TWENTY-TWO

The next day, the rail company's official inquiry into the acts of sabotage took place, and I was called to support George Burley's evidence. But there was little they could do, except record that the events had happened, unless Johnson turned up, which seemed unlikely. As for Sheridan's death, since the family had made no complaint to the rail company, then it was not their business: it would have to go to a proper court of law.

I asked George to come in uniform to the races tomorrow, and gave him a pass from Nell to get into Exhibition Park for the event. Then we parted, and I went to a doctor about my shoulder, which had not yet begun to improve.

He looked at me over his glasses and asked whether it hurt when I coughed.

'It hurts when I do practically anything, as a matter of fact,' I answered.

He checked me over, and then declared that I had a broken shoulder-blade. He bandaged me up tightly so that it would heal, but I wouldn't let him bandage my arm to my side: I

The doctor checked me over, bandaged me up and put my arm in a sling, so that it would heal.

was hoping to use my arms in Hawaii. But he insisted on a **sling**.

I asked the doctor for a proper medical report about my broken shoulder, and he gave it to me.

That evening, Bill Baudelaire arrived from Toronto, and then Catto from England. We had a meeting in my hotel room. An eyebrow or two was raised at my sling, but I had already told them about my midnight fight with Johnson, so they asked no questions about it. Catto had brought some papers with him.

'It was a good guess of yours, Tor, that the report on the cats which you found in Filmer's briefcase had come from a computer printer. The Master of the College had a call from Mercer Lorrimore this morning – well, this morning in English time – giving permission for him to tell us everything. So now we have a copy of the official college report on the affair, and the **vet**'s report too.'

He showed the papers to me and Baudelaire. 'What we don't know, however,' he continued, 'is how on earth Filmer came into possession of a copy of the college report.'

'It would be neat if we could find out,' I said. 'It would enable us to tie things up better tomorrow.'

'One of my men is working on it,' Catto said. 'I'll telephone him before tomorrow's meeting to see if he's got any news for us. I think we've got him anyway, but we'll need all the evidence and the help we can get.'

◆

Julius Apollo Filmer walked into the private conference room at Exhibition Park the next day expecting to receive official notice that Laurentide Ice was now his and would run in his name alone in the afternoon's race.

When he entered, the two Directors of Security were

sitting at the end of the conference table, with other senior members of the Canadian Jockey Club beside them. They were there as witnesses. Bill Baudelaire and Valentine Catto were seated at the table, facing the door by which Filmer would enter.

There were two doors into the room – the one Filmer entered by, and another one which led to a small kitchen, where I was waiting with three other people. As soon as Filmer arrived, I went along the passage, locked the door he had come in by, and put the key into my pocket. Then I returned and took my place behind the other door.

A microphone on the table was connected to a tape re- corder, and also enabled those of us in the kitchen to hear what was being said in the conference room.

We heard Bill Baudelaire's deep voice greeting Filmer and inviting him to sit at the table opposite himself and Catto. 'You know Brigadier Catto, of course,' Bill said.

As the two men had looked in anger at each other on many occasions, especially that day in court in England, then yes, he knew Catto.

'And these gentlemen are officials of the Canadian Jockey Club,' Bill went on; I imagined him pointing down the table.

'What *is* this?' Filmer asked. 'All I want are my official papers about Laurentide Ice.'

The Brigadier said, 'We're taking this opportunity of making a first investigation into some racing matters, and it seemed best to do it now, as so many of the people involved are in Vancouver at this time.'

'What are you talking about?' asked Filmer.

'We should explain,' the Brigadier continued smoothly, 'that we are recording what is said in this room this morning. This is not a formal trial, but what is said here may be repeated at any trial in the future. We would ask you to remember this.'

Filmer said strongly, 'I object to this. You can't do this; I'm not staying.' But he found the door locked, of course.

'Let me out,' Filmer said. He was angry now. 'You can't do this.'

In the kitchen Mercer Lorrimore took a deep breath, opened the door to the conference room, went through and closed it behind him.

CHAPTER TWENTY-THREE

'Good morning, Julius,' Mercer said.

'What are you doing here?' Filmer's voice was surprised, but not disturbed. 'Tell them to give me my papers and be done with it.'

'Sit down, Julius,' said Mercer. There was the noise of chair legs on carpet.

'This inquiry, Mr Filmer,' Baudelaire said, 'is principally concerned with your actions before and during the journey of the Race Train. Mr Lorrimore, please would you proceed?'

Mercer cleared his throat. 'My son Sheridan,' he said calmly, 'who died two days ago, suffered from a mental illness that caused him to do odd – and sometimes horrible – things.'

There was a pause, but no words from Filmer. I admired Mercer's courage in saying all this.

'In May, in Cambridge, England, Sheridan . . . he killed some animals. On the train, Julius, you indicated that you knew about this unfortunate event, and you plainly hinted that you would use this knowledge as a lever to persuade me and my family to give you our horse, Voting Right.'

Brigadier Catto took up the story. 'We found out only an hour ago how this piece of information came into your

79

possession, Mr Filmer. It was a pure accident. One of your horses happened to die in Newmarket, which is near Cambridge. The vet who investigated the cause of your horse's death sent you a report about his findings. By mistake, his secretary also printed an extra page off the computer and sent it to you. It contained a report about the killing of some cats in a Cambridge college.'

'This is rubbish!' exclaimed Filmer.

'You kept this extra report,' the Brigadier went on. 'For a person like yourself, such information contains great possibilities – for blackmail. If only you could find out whom the report was about. Then one day, you read in the local newspaper that Mercer Lorrimore was putting up money for a new college library. You would only have to ask one question to find out that Mercer Lorrimore's son had left that college in a hurry during May. But no one would say why he had left. You became sure that the vet's report was relevant to Sheridan Lorrimore's departure. You did nothing with this knowledge until you heard that Mercer Lorrimore would be on the Transcontinental Race Train, and then you saw an opportunity for blackmailing Mr Lorrimore into letting you have his horse, Voting Right.'

'You can't prove any of this,' Filmer spat out.

'We all believe,' said Bill Baudelaire's voice, 'that although you are rich enough to buy your own horses, there is something in you that makes you desire to crush people.'

'Spare me the moral speech,' Filmer said. 'If you haven't got any proof, just shut up.'

'Very well,' said Baudelaire. 'Would our next visitor please come in?'

◆

Daffodil Quentin had been listening with growing anger. She opened the door to the conference room and stormed in. That left only George and myself in the kitchen.

'You horrible crook,' we heard Daffodil shout. 'I'll never give you or sell you my half of Laurentide Ice, and you can threaten and blackmail until you're blue in the face. You can try to frighten my groom, but from now on you can't frighten me. I think you're beneath contempt, and should be put in a zoo.'

Bill Baudelaire, who had persuaded her to come with him to Vancouver, cleared his throat and sounded as if he were trying not to laugh.

'Mrs Quentin,' he said, 'is prepared to be a witness . . .'

'You bet I am,' Daffodil interrupted.

'. . . to the fact that you threatened to have her put on trial for killing one of her own horses if she didn't give you her share of Laurentide Ice.'

'You used me,' Daffodil said angrily. 'You bought your way on to the train and you were charming, but all you were aiming to do was get close to Mercer Lorrimore so that you could try to crush him and cause him pain and take away his horse. You make me sick.'

CHAPTER TWENTY-FOUR

There was a short silence after Daffodil's outburst. Then Filmer said, 'I don't have to listen to this.'

'I'm afraid you do,' said Baudelaire. 'We have here a letter from Mrs Quentin's insurance company, written yesterday, saying that they fully investigated the matter of the horse, called Thunder, that died, and are satisfied that they paid her claim correctly. We also have a statement from Mrs Quentin's former groom, Lenny Higgs, to the effect that you learned about Thunder's death and the special food for Laurentide Ice on one of your early visits to the horse-car on the train. He goes on to swear that he was later frightened into saying that Mrs Quentin gave him some food to give to Thunder. The insurance company, as you have heard, are satisfied that even if Mrs Quentin did give Thunder some special food, it was not the cause of his death. Higgs further swears that the man who frightened him, by telling him he would be sent to prison where he would be beaten up, and stabbed, is a former railwayman called Alex Mitchell McLachlan.'

'*What*?' For the first time there was fear in Filmer's voice, and I found it sweet.

'Yes. Higgs recognized him from this photograph.' There was a pause while Baudelaire showed Filmer the photograph. 'This man travelled in the racegoers' part of the train under the name of Johnson. We have by now shown the photograph to plenty of current and former railwaymen, and lots of them have said that he is McLachlan.'

There was silence where Filmer might have spoken.

'You were observed speaking to McLachlan . . .'

'Yes, by me too,' Daffodil interrupted again. 'It was at Thunder Bay, and I didn't like the look of him. You used him to frighten Lenny, and you told me Lenny would be a witness in court against me . . . I didn't know you'd frightened the boy. You told me he hated me and would be glad to tell lies about me . . .' She could hardly breathe from anger. 'I don't know how you can live with yourself.'

'Thank you,' said Baudelaire, to control her outburst. 'Now we come, Mr Filmer, to the matter of your attempt to wreck the train. Would you please come in, Mr Burley?'

I smiled at George. 'We're on,' I said, removing my coat. 'After you.'

He and I went through the door. He was in his conductor's uniform, and I was dressed in my waiter's grey trousers, white shirt, yellow waistcoat and striped tie – the perfect waiter, apart from my sling. This was the first time the Brigadier and Baudelaire had seen me in waiter's uniform, and their mouths dropped open. They hadn't appreciated how perfect a disguise it was.

'Oh, that's who you are!' exclaimed Daffodil to me. 'I couldn't recognize you outside, when you were wearing a coat.'

Mercer patted her hand and gave me the faintest of smiles over her head. Filmer's face was dark and tense.

'Would you come forward, please,' Bill Baudelaire said. 'The conductor, Mr George Burley, yesterday gave the railway company a report about three acts of sabotage on the Race Train. Fortunately, disaster was avoided on all three occasions, but we believe that all these dangerous situations were the work of Alex McLachlan and that he was acting on your instructions and was paid by you.'

'No,' said Filmer, dully.

'Our inquiries are not yet complete,' Baudelaire said, 'but we do know that the railway offices in Montreal were visited a couple of weeks before the Race Train trip by a man who looked like you. This man said that he was writing a book about industrial sabotage. He asked for, and was given, a list of names of former railway workers who had performed acts of sabotage — so that he could interview them for his book, he said.'

Baudelaire had already told me that this list should, of course, never have been given out, and that the person who did so had been sacked.

'McLachlan's name was on that list,' Baudelaire said.

Filmer said nothing, but the realization of defeat was beginning to show on his face.

CHAPTER TWENTY-FIVE

Baudelaire continued with an account of the three acts of sabotage. He explained to the meeting that the first – the unhitching of the Lorrimores' car at Cartier, before Winnipeg – should never have happened. Filmer had mixed up Winnipeg and Vancouver and told McLachlan to sabotage the train before Winnipeg, when he meant before Vancouver. The second – the stealing of the heating fuel – could have caused the death of some of the horses from the cold. The third was not part of Filmer's plan, and Filmer had tried to stop McLachlan; but by then McLachlan was out of control and just wanted his revenge against the railway company.

Filmer began to protest, but Bill Baudelaire interrupted him. Baudelaire told the full story of the overheating axle and George being knocked out and tied up, the radio being broken, and McLachlan waiting up the track for whoever would be sent with flares to warn the Canadian.

This was the first time Filmer had heard these details, and he stared darkly into space, seeing a miserable future for himself.

'McLachlan did attack the man with the flares,' Baudelaire continued, 'but by good fortune failed to knock him out. It was this man here who was sent with the flares.' He nodded in my direction. 'He succeeded in lighting the flares and stopping the Canadian. You, Mr Filmer, are responsible with McLachlan for all these acts of sabotage.'

'No.' Filmer's voice was a rising shout of protest. 'I told him not to; I didn't want him to.'

His lawyers would love that confession, I thought, when they listened to the tape.

'McLachlan's attack on Mr Kelsey here was serious,' Baudelaire went on. He picked up the report the doctor had given me. 'In addition to hurting the conductor, McLachlan broke this waiter's shoulder-blade. Mr Kelsey has seen the photograph of McLachlan, and recognizes the man who attacked him.'

Filmer was sweating now. He was on the edge.

'We will take you to court for all these crimes,' Baudelaire said in conclusion.

That was when Filmer lost control. He came up out of his chair fighting mad, driven to hurting somebody – anybody – in revenge for his defeat.

I was the one he chose. He couldn't have known how important I had actually been in causing his defeat, that I had been his real enemy all along. No, he probably saw me as the least important of the people there, only a waiter, one he could hurt without being punished for it.

But I saw him coming. I also saw the alarm on the Brigadier's face and understood that, if I fought back, as instinct was insisting I should – if I did to Filmer the sort of damage I had told the Brigadier I had done to McLachlan – then Filmer would be in a stronger position in court.

Thought before action, as the Brigadier would say.

In the short time it took for Filmer to reach me, all these thoughts went through my mind, and I had made my decision. I didn't fight back, although every muscle in my body was ready for action.

I rolled my head a little sideways and he hit me twice, quite hard, on the cheek and the chin. I fell back with a crash against the wall (which didn't do my shoulder much good) and slid down the wall until I was sitting on the floor.

Filmer was standing over me, getting ready to hit me again, when George Burley and Bill Baudelaire grabbed hold of him and pulled him away.

The Brigadier pressed a button on the table, which soon

resulted in the arrival of two large policemen, who took Filmer away. One might almost have felt pity for him – until one remembered that groom lying murdered in an English ditch.

Daffodil Quentin's eyes were wide with concern as she came over to where I was still sitting on the floor. 'You poor boy,' she said. 'How perfectly awful!!'

'Mr Burley,' Bill said smoothly, 'would you be so kind as to take Mrs Quentin to the reception room downstairs, where you will find the other owners. Lunch will be served there shortly . . . and please do stay yourself for lunch. We will take care of Mr Kelsey.'

George took Daffodil away, but not before she had murmured 'You poor boy' once or twice more.

When they had left, the Brigadier switched off the tape recorder. 'Poor boy indeed!' he said. 'You chose to let him hit you; I saw you.'

'He couldn't!' Mercer protested. 'No one can do that, surely.'

'He could and he did,' the Brigadier said. 'It was brilliant, quick thinking.' He helped me to my feet.

'Did you really?' Mercer asked.

I nodded, gently touching my injured face.

'I sent him on the train,' the Brigadier said, 'to stop Filmer doing whatever he was planning.' He smiled. 'It was a sort of match – a two-horse race.'

'It seems to have been a close thing now and again,' Mercer commented.

'Perhaps,' said the Brigadier, 'but our runner had the edge.'

CHAPTER TWENTY-SIX

Mercer Lorrimer felt that he couldn't attend the party so soon after his son's death. The President of Exhibition Park understood, and let him use his private room, which was next to the reception room, and offered just as splendid a view of the racetrack.

Mercer had asked if I would join him and I accepted. So there we were, drinking champagne and talking about Filmer.

'I liked him, you know,' said Mercer, surprised at himself.

'Yes, he could be very charming. That was one of his main tools.'

'He even told me about the trial back in England. He insisted he was innocent, and told me that he didn't think any the worse of the Jockey Club.'

'In fact,' I said, 'he was eaten up by hatred for the Jockey Club. He threatened to get his revenge, and McLachlan was to be the instrument of his revenge.'

'What was the real point of this morning?' Mercer asked.

'Last time he got off by frightening the witnesses,' I explained. 'So this time we thought we would act quickly, and get the evidence down on tape, before he'd had a chance to frighten anyone else.'

'Did you think I could be frightened, then?' asked Mercer.

'You don't know Filmer. He could have threatened to hurt Xanthe or Bambi. One of the witnesses in the trial in England changed his story after Filmer's man told him, in detail, what would happen to his young daughter if he gave evidence in the trial.'

'Dear God,' said Mercer. 'Surely he'll be sent to prison.'

'Perhaps. At least he'll be warned off the horse-racing world, which is how he makes a living. So we'll have hurt him.'

(As a matter of fact, both Filmer and McLachlan − when he was found − were sent to prison. But that was months ahead.)

The race was just about to start. Mercer's Voting Right led from the start. He seemed to have started too fast, however, and for a while, both Laurentide Ice (who was running in Mrs Quentin's name alone) and Sparrowgrass were closing the gap. Then Laurentide Ice melted away, as Mrs Baudelaire had said he would, and the race was between Sparrowgrass and Voting Right. Sparrowgrass made a great effort to catch the other horse up, and Voting Right was starting to tire, but it was still Voting Right who was a neck ahead at the finishing line.

His horse's splendid victory gave Mercer fresh energy. He turned to me and said, 'Thank you. Thank you for all you have done.'

Just then, the President came into the room to congratulate Mercer. He showed us that if we pulled aside the curtains that were covering one wall of the room, we could see into the reception room. 'They can't see you,' he explained. 'It's one-way glass.'

We stood and watched the party for a while. There were all the familiar faces – the Youngs, the Unwins . . .

The President turned to me and said that he'd heard that I was a bit of a hero. He asked if there was anything he could do for me.

I smiled. 'As a matter of fact, yes, there is,' I said. 'Do you see that young woman next door, with the fair hair and the worried look on her face?'

'Nell Richmond,' Mercer said.

'Would you mind if she came in here for a while?' I asked.

'Not at all,' said the President, and within minutes he could be seen talking to her. He couldn't have told her who to expect in his room, however, because when she came in and saw me, she was surprised – and happy.

'You're on your feet! Daffodil said the waiter was badly

hurt.' Her voice died away and she swallowed. 'I was afraid . . .'

'That we wouldn't get to Hawaii?'

'Oh.' It was somewhere between a laugh and a cry. 'You . . . !'

'Yes?

She looked through the one-way glass and said that she had to be in there with the others: that was her job. 'And talking of my job,' she said, 'read this after I've gone.' She gave me a piece of paper which she'd been looking for in her handbag.

She went out without looking back and I unfolded the paper. It was a message from the boss of her travel company. It told her that she could have two weeks' holiday, starting immediately, and ended, 'Have a good time.'

I closed my eyes.

'What's the matter?' asked Mercer, concerned. He'd been about to go to receive his horse's prize.

I opened my eyes. The letter still had the same message. I showed it to him and he read it.

'I dare say that Brigadier Catto will match that,' he said.

'He'd better,' I replied. 'If he doesn't, I'll resign.'

EXERCISES

Vocabulary Work

Look back at the 'Dictionary Words' in this book.

1 The following groups of words are connected with one of the Dictionary Words. Which word is each group connected with? (The first one has been done for you.)

a danger, damage, train: *sabotage*

b drink, alcohol, celebrate

c train, warning, bright light

d animal, sick, doctor

e leather, locked, newspaper cuttings

f threaten, secret, money

2 Find words to match these definitions:

a a person who looks after horses

b a deep valley with very steep sides

c a metal bar that connects a pair of wheels on a vehicle

d one of the sections into which some railway carriages are divided

e a river of ice that moves slowly down a valley

f quiet and bad-tempered

3 Write sentences with these words, to show their meanings clearly.

a *bedridden*   e *unhitch*

b *expelled*   f *persecute*

c *transcontinental*   g *waistcoat*

d *sling* (noun)   h *brochure*

Comprehension

Chapters 1–5

1 In the Transcontinental Race Train:

a where was the dining car?

b which carriages held the luggage, horses and grooms?

c where were the owners' sleeping-compartments?

2 How did Tor become an investigator for the Jockey Club?

3 Where did most of Mercer Lorrimore's money come from?

Chapters 6–10

4 Are these sentences true (√) or false (x)?

a The Lorrimores' carriage was unhitched at Cartier.

b Julius Filmer is always confusing Ottowa and Vancouver.

c Sheridan Lorrimore was expelled from Oxford University.

d Canada has a single railway track across most of it.

Chapters 11–15

5 Answer these questions.

a What did Tor do so that he could spend some time in Filmer's compartment without making anyone suspicious?

b Why did Tor have to go at least half a mile back down the track to stop the Canadian?

Chapters 16–20

6 Put these sentences in the right order.

a George was tied up, and had a cloth, fixed down with sticky tape, filling his mouth so that he couldn't cry out.

b Lorrimore wanted the train stopped so that he could go back and try to find his son.

c The conductor of the Canadian said that he would radio ahead to Kamploops.

Chapters 21–26

7 Who said these things?

a 'He killed two cats like that when he was fourteen, in our garden.'

b 'If you haven't got any proof, just shut up.'

c 'I think you're beneath contempt, and should be put into a zoo.'

Discussion

1 Why do you think horse-racing is often linked with crime?
2 Why is it difficult to prove that someone is guilty of blackmail? What would you do if *you* were blackmailed by someone?

Writing

1 Write an advertisement for the Race Train. Use a map of Canada to describe the route of the train across the country.
2 Look at the picture on page 24. In 150 words, describe Xanthe and how she is feeling at that moment.

Review

1 Why do you think the author decided to use Tor Kelsey as the person to tell the story? Does it make it more exciting to see the story through just one person's eyes?
2 Write a review of the book (200 words).